Keeper of the Town

by

Don Cameron

Tales and stories
connecting us all
to the deep ancestry
within.

Published by

Savage PRESS
Box 115, Superior, WI 54880 (715) 394-9513

First Edition
Published in 1996
by
Savage Press
PO Box 115
Superior, WI. 54880

All the characters in this book are fictitious. Any resemblance to actual persons, living or dead, is purely coincidental. The names, incidents, dialogue and opinions expressed are products of the author's imagination and are not to be construed as real.

ISBN # 1-886028-15-X
Library of Congress Catalog Card Number 96-067505

All artwork by Dale Hagen, Duluth, MN

Printed in the United States of America
By Morris Publishing, Kearney, NE.

Acknowledgments

The process of writing is solitary confinement in a room full of ghosts. You see them, you hear them, you listen, and what they say and do becomes a story.

But for stories to become a book is another matter. This process involves readers and critics and artists and proofers and editors and printers and, in the end, these collective energies are dear friends and family. I owe so much to so many.

Most important of all, is the Algonquin Breakfast Club of the North members who took time to read, critique, suggest and be a constant source of encouragement as well as work-in-progress editors who, in placing honesty above friendship, were far more than cheerleaders. Without these fine friends this book would not have happened. A special thanks to Professor John Paul Schifsky, English Department, College of St. Scholastica. To him fell the laborious task of proofing and much footwork in urging the project to completion. And, of course, to Mike of Savage Press who read and had faith. A special thanks to you all.

Don Cameron

Preface

There is this urge to tell stories," Harry said. "People gather, and the stories begin."

"Everyone has a history," his friend replied. "Everyone comes from somewhere."

"–Like having a long string of grandparents–"

"Something like that. But stories are more than tales, Harry. I think–I think they connect us."

To Aimee, Micheal and David, three little people who finally made a grandfather out of me.

Table of Contents

1 Keeper of the Town

Money in his pockets, places to spend it and no timetable to intrude upon his habits. Cruising the Avenue as he always had—shiny brogans, slick serge trousers, a chesterfield flung open with a white silk scarf swinging free about his neck, a prized malacca crooked over one forearm and a black Homburg cocked jauntily over one dark brow—only the callboy knew where to find him if a train were being made up. Even then, a hostler helper coaxed the giant steam engine down the spur to the coal chutes and water tower to fill the tenders before an ore run, and there was time for another tale, another hand of cribbage, one more beer. If the cribbage was good the beer was free; if not, the beer fell to a running tab which he seldom paid, it being the civic contribution of tavern owners who were as bold about collecting as Herman was about evading. As a railroad engineer he earned a generous wage, which he banked, and which thereafter was of no value to him beyond his modest life-style and creditors' demands. The cash he did carry was merely a symbolic link to his unknown wealth and was never offered as a hedge against the credit he expected as his due. These small oversights concerning debt were about proportionate to his general contempt for money, for, while he always owed five dollars to some bar patron along the Avenue, he loaned great sums to local businesses from which he neither begged interest nor called in a debt. As a community investment, these loans were simply forgotten, and his innocence about such matters was often the borrower's torment.

He could account for thirty years of the same, allowing for certain errors in the telling, but never had he imagined the railroad would shut down. He did say to a young fireman one time, "Some day they'll push buttons to run this whole operation and you'll be out of a job," as more or less a threat to insure proper care for the magnificent machinery.

In those days Herman saw no further than the bend in track or a downgrade into the switch yards with the wheels of a hundred ore cars squealing and smoldering and climbing the rails. When at the end of an ore run he shouted tie-up orders to the hostler coming aboard, who with head bobbing assent wished to hell that Herman would go away, it was "Treat this ol' darlin' right or you'll be out of a job." Any hostler understood that "this ol' darlin'" was the 215 Mallet, the world's largest and most powerful steam engine, and understood well that Herman's affection for the engine was a reasonable warning which had little to do with management or company loyalty.

Later, when he changed out of his work clothes and hit the Avenue, he expected that same commitment from shopkeepers along the way. It was "Dress up them show windows. Smile. Put some sales on. Who the hell knows what you got in them boxes over there?" his voice relentless and grating on ears throughout the shops. He knew nothing about business but everything about customers, which left shopkeepers with one defense: "You buying, Herman?" "Promoting," he'd say, and go on to sweep snow from doorways, shovel walks, salt patches of ice and curse those who cuffed new snow onto his efforts. No one knew how it all began, nor could anyone remember it being otherwise, but just as they accepted the consequence of winter, people accepted and expected no less from Herman.

What they could remember was no longer an embarrassment to him. His sons, grown and with families of their own, had long ago removed to distant places, while his wife Myrna had long ago moved away with another man. He had anguished over this and had finally abandoned the tiny house Myrna kept so neatly to take a single room at the YMCA near his railroad.

But now as the passing of years swept him into retirement he knew he had grandchildren somewhere, though he could not fit their tiny faces to tiny bodies. But this was no concern to him for he reasoned that tiny faces were universal and that all old people were grandparents, a conclusion that preserved a sense of continuity so vital to his bachelorhood. It was natural, too, that he should often join hands with kids on the street, sing a song and jig and swing his cane to their delight. Older children laughed and mocked him, unaware that these spirited moments sprang from Herman's cherished memories of his own youth.

It was also natural that when the impact of the shutdown settled over the town, and disbelief gave in to anger and then finally to a collective numbness, Herman was the first to cry out, "What about our kids?"

"What kids," many scoffed. "All you got here is yourself." But neither that truth nor the shutdown altered his style.

One day that winter of 1954 he made a last call to the end of the Avenue where, wrapped casually against the cold, he examined the railroad yards now abandoned to a blanketing of snow. The ghostly silhouettes of rail ties and rails and axles and wheels and plates and spikes, the railbeds that wandered among the roundhouse and carshop and turntable and down to the water tower and coal chute—all of this now a cold and quiet portrait—filled him with disgust. To his left, the high ore docks reached out into the bay, waiting for the Edna G. to tow an ore boat into the slip. He could almost hear the bells and whistles and wheels and the metal of ore cars rolling to their positions over dumping pockets, the chutes grinding downward to holds beneath the deck of the boats, and then the ore-punchers coaxing raw ore to slide down the chutes into the holds. Above all others, he remembered the sound of the ore-puncher poles as they knocked against the stubborn matrix of ore, the uneven rhythms echoing over the town, urging the people to spend their earnings in the taverns and pool halls and shops and the Scandinavian Co-op Mercantile, the Company Store. It was one great seasonal symphony that people automatically obeyed but had long ceased to hear.

Now, in the absence of that symphony was the quiet. That alone rang in his ears. From anywhere on the Avenue he could look back and see the red brick office building, its unscrubbed windows bewildered and blinking at a baleful winter sun. It had been the gateway to the diamonds where ore cars were graded and switched before rolling out onto the docks. In here the call lists were made up and the ore runs scheduled and the tonnage recorded; in this building the entire railroad was kept in order quite apart from the town which ran on its own energy of well-being. Now it reminded him of his sad little house that stood empty near Skunk Creek at the center of town. "It's always too late," he murmured, and for the first time in almost forty years he felt utterly alone. He stepped to the gate and handled the lock, pulling at it and rolling it in the palm of his hand, trying to remember details, to go back and review his life on the railroad, a life that seemed now to be concluding itself with this humiliation. But his mind refused. Instead, it swung adamantly toward the future, and all at once he stepped back and shouted, "Go to hell!"

In the pool hall on the Avenue, squat, grim Doulas stood behind the bar polishing a glass. "You don' see it come, Herman?" A yellowed tongue packed a stub of cigar into one corner of his mouth and a pencil line of spittle drained down a crease in his fat chin. "Soon is old pipple like you, Herman, like me. Is long time like this," he said as Herman pondered the quiet on the Avenue. "You got pool hall, you notice—is no war, is no business," he added.

"What's war got to do with it?"

"Is make Doulas rich. Is make Herman number one hoghead on railroad."

"Ten years ago, for chrissake. The war was over ten years ago."

"Is no war, is no business," Doulas insisted, wiping at the counter and humming as though at peace with himself. He paused, set the glass down, hoisted his trousers and mumbled to himself. "Doulas is burn the joint down and collect the insuring."

Who knows what stirs a man to action, but usually, tiny as

the mosquito bite, it stings a heap of vague grievances and robs a man's logic. Herman swung about, the Homburg crouched over one leering eye and charged from the window to bend himself tightly over the counter, his face pushed at the enemy. "You sonofabitch," he whispered. "You goddamned Greek."

"Is has been, Herman—"

"How much you figure I spent here over the years?"

"Railroad, she—"

"To hell with the railroad! Throw some lights on! Shine them windows! Clean up the place and business as usual, goddamit!"

At Millard's furniture store it was the same. The mute old were gathered about the heat register cut in the warped wood flooring. They looked up when Herman entered, then turned away. There was the sweet smell of rot, and Herman remembered why he seldom stopped here. Old Man Penson had the usual urine drops on his trousers, and on his vest were breakfast scraps and smudges, and the slivers of froth at the corners of his mouth made that great head on frail shoulders look like a horse's snout. Fat Matt Settergren sat hunched on a stool. He blinked nervously and his mustache twitched in rhythm to his club-like fingers drumming on the cluttered desk that had long since been abandoned by proprietor Millard. At the same time, Old Millard, in a rocker with hooped rungs, was himself limp in the tent-of-shirt he wore. With two bony fingers pressed at his larynx to relieve the crackling in his throat as he breathed, he stared into the gloom, leaving Fat Matt's mindless drumming of his fingers the only sign of life. "Goddamn," Herman muttered. There was nothing to say to ghosts.

From there he went on to pass the dime store, and the shoe store where Olley would be cutting merchandise prices to the nearest round number, and the Beacon Tavern where Cully Yohan would be starting his day with black coffee and cold fish cakes. Cully's complaint was consistent: "Is it yoost me, or tough all over?" a refrain that endured good and bad times alike, and Herman was in no mood for Cully.

But he did pause at the drugstore corner to look back at the Avenue, at the winter sun hanging over the empty roundhouse and carshop now sunk deeply in the whiteness. A sadness clutched at him and drove him around the corner and up the street toward Adam the barber.

"Adam!" he shouted. "Adam!"

"A fine morning for grog, Little Mother!" Adam shouted through his muffler without looking up. Taking a final swipe at the snow on the walk, he led the way inside the shop. Adam was hunched and gaunt from a lifetime of excesses that he did not regret. He reached among the tonics and withdrew a certain bottle, snatched two cups from the shelf below, poured generously into both, and dropped himself into the barber's chair. "Good as Grandma Lake's moonshine," he laughed, remembering their youth with reverence. "The good ol' days, Little Mother. We'll drink to that."

"We're always too late," Herman said. He had taken his usual place on the bench near the window and was studying the street.

"Too late? Too late for what? You miss the good ol' days Little Mother, the booze and women and Stutz Bearcat—?"

"The town, dammit! We gotta do something to keep the kids!"

"What kids?" Adam asked, then added affectionately, "They'll be all right. Folks will keep the old town going."

"Old people die, Adam."

"Nothing is forever, Little Mother."

"We never by-gawd thought that."

"Ya, ya," Adam said, dismissing the subject. He fell silent then. He turned to stir the coals in the stove, then twisted about, grunting as he refilled the cups. Now and then he breathed a noisy sigh in an attempt at conversation. Finally he said, "Me and the ol' lady—me and the ol' lady—we're going south."

"We're going south," he said again.

"For the winter?"

"For good."

"You sonofabitch."

"Ya, ya. And I'm the meanest, most ugliest man in the world when I tell you this, too." Again he fell silent, reached for the bottle, thought better of that and sank back into the chair. For a long while, looking aimlessly about the shop he pondered the risk of truth. Finally he said, "Roth's closing out, too."

Already on his feet, Herman dashed his cup to the bench, lunged for the door, pulled it hard open and shot through to the street. "And screw going south!" he shouted back.

He faltered on a patch of ice and angry reflex sent the cane to his hand while he caught himself and livened his step. Adam's words were on his mind and he was oblivious to all else until he burst into the Scandinavian Co-op Mercantile store and climbed the stairs to Roth's office.

Roth stood behind the broad oak desk, a gift from the Railroad during better times. The desk was uncluttered, in Roth's style, Roth who wore a dark suit buttoned and proper with a four-in-hand tie tucked neatly inside his vest. With his hands clasped before himself, he had calmly anticipated Herman's visit. "You'll get your money out of the business," he said quietly.

"To hell with the money. What about business? You close down and sure as hell you tear the roots out of this town!" Herman cried. "Hell, the first settling of this town began with this store and it's been the meeting place for every generation of kids since!"

"I know. I know."

"Then put some sales on. Run some of them lost leaders, bamboozle the public and to hell with the railroad!"

"It was good to you, Herman."

"I can't remember."

"Come, come, now." Roth's eyes scanned the ceiling, the pattern of clover leaf in the embossed tin and the obvious seams where nail heads had pulled through, the forest of droplights and pull cords and cash trollies that had once zipped along taut cables to and from the bank of windows in the accounting office overlooking the sales floor. "When times were good," he said, "–what you see down there was all right–but you know what it takes nowadays?" He paused, waiting for Herman to see the reality or to interrupt and, when he did not, Roth continued on. "The Railroad's not to blame, Herman—give or take some politics."

"It closed down, dammit!"

"Regrouping, I suppose."

"It can't pack up the yards and haul them away."

"They're expendable, of course," Roth said patiently. "But go back a little, Herman. The Railroad built the town for its own use. We can both remember Company housing and Company heating and power and telephone—and how many homes are built on old rail ties, and in how many basements will you find Company shovels and wheel barrows and other small pieces of Company property? It's been easy and we were willing dependents."

"The Company owed the people that much."

"And the YMCA that you live in? We were all too comfortable, Herman."

"Then we make changes. We make them now!"

Roth smiled. "There you have it, Herman. Trends. Progress. Change." He noted Herman's brogans, the cane on his forearm and the Homburg cocked menacingly over that one eye. Nothing about Herman had changed in forty years. "You retired dreamily," Roth said, "and I stayed on here—both of us certain it would always be the same." He chuckled at the irony. "Remember old man Elliot—gray hat, sharp gray suit too small at the shoulders like a school boy's first suit, a fresh carnation in the lapel and tidy as a Wall Street banker—?"

"And Bill St. Maries and Alec Holiday and Morris Van Valkenberg and St. Johns—I knew them all."

"We thought they were antiques."

"But the town's still here."

"And on wheels. This store is past its prime just like natural ore, which was our bread and butter—with this new taconite ore replacing us just thirty miles up the shore—"

"That's it! That's it!" Herman cried. "Another goddamned company town!"

"And people there will become dependent just like we were."

"We'll do it without them. We'll keep the town going. We need kids building houses and raising families!"

"And what do we offer them?"

The reply stopped Herman. He stood exhausted and resentful as he eyed Roth, trying to understand this man of logic, his friend, this man in charge of an old landmark and the town's oldest continuing business. Hell, this building was old when he and Roth were kids. "I give you this, Roth. You're a negative sonofabitch." He turned to the door, and for a moment stood framed in the bleak stair light. "I hate like hell being buried nowhere."

On the street. Narrow footpath. Snow escalating in doorways and basement windows. Wind hurling more white. Wind hurling memories—Myrna with white white breasts and red cheeks and flaming eyes—she stood in the kitchen screaming "You think this can go on forever? Whiskey! Whiskey! Whiskey! You're just like your father—crazy like your father, you and Adam—you're both crazy!" And then one day she was gone and he had buried his head in her pillows, sucking at the fragrance of her. He had cried. On the kitchen table were groceries he had brought home to this empty house, not that he'd known they were needed nor what to buy, but because his sense of guilt demanded something. He would not have thought about flowers for Myrna. He had never thought about flowers for Myrna. While living with her he did not know what he had done nor what to repair nor how to repair it, thus his guilt was a feeling and not something he understood, even when

Myrna made her final and damning departure. Resolving that was just the notion that he had always been a bachelor who lived apart from Myrna and family, like a bull walrus with no function other than for mating. He felt little humiliation or remorse about this, other than knowing he had created his own irrelevancy. His decision not to pursue her was the acceptance of a life-style he had always lived. And he moved from the little house.

Still, he returned frequently to clean and repair and put things in order. This was a new sense of duty, to make up for all he had neglected to do before, as though a curse hung over him. At intervals he repainted as well, never once altering the white with yellow trim and matching shutters. The fence was white, too, enclosing a neatly trimmed lawn and a small garden where the land sloped to Skunk creek over which a narrow foot bridge crossed to the street. All this he continued to do over the years as a contract with the past, the genius of it a kind of virtue that delivered him happily into retirement.

The beer sign squeaking over his head interrupted his thoughts. Charlie Forbes' place. Entering, Herman knew it was more a habit with him than a need. Charlie's head sat on overstuffed shoulders like a huge ball. He wore a crew-cut and conducted business from a wrestler's body. The tavern had been the Golden Gate when Zotis lived, but now it lacked the rancor and charm that the humorless Zotis had given it.

"You need a new sign over the doorway, Charlie," Herman announced, "maybe some soft lights along that wall over there, some clean tables with linens where them booths are. Booths are for people in a hurry. Tables are for visiting—."

"Who the hell bought this place?" Charlie asked. He shook the rinse water from a beer glass and put it down, then swiped at his nose and placed two barrel-like fists on the bar. "Chrissakes, Herman—"

"Zotis kept pool tables racked up," Herman went on, "a couple of games going in the back and some whores in the rooms overhead." He looked up and jabbed his cane at the ceiling. "Didn't know about the whores, didja, Charlie? Booze, games, and women—all in one stop. Hell, wasn't standing room on the street."

"Too much horseshit," Charlie said, reaching for a cigarette and lighting it while he eyed Herman with mild contempt.

"Packards and Willys and Knights," Herman said, stepping to the bar. "I'll have a beer, Charlie—yessir, twelve beer joints from here down to Whiskey Row where you found twelve more—three boarding houses with a bunch of fancy girls along the way. Them were the days, Charlie. The railroad was young. The town was young. Everybody was young—and the town had vigor!"

"You old guys," Charlie said. "Yer all grave diggers."

"So now we got twelve churches and two saloons—you and Cully—" Herman put the beer to his lips, and remembering it all, sucked with ecstasy. "See how it is, Charlie—a town gets respect and loses its vigor." He turned and strode to the door.

"Hey!" Charlie shouted. "Who pays for the beer?"

"Zotis," Herman said. "The sonofabitch owed me money when he died."

Adam the Barber was going south, Herman murmured to himself. He was extra. Both of them were extra. Both of them were part of another time, and while the joyous memory filled his mind, his town was fading away. "We were willing dependents," Roth said, to a system that was huge, unmovable and that had seemed eternal. Herman was angry with himself now, because he realized that to him the town had consisted of places and events more than it had consisted of names and faces—all vague to him now, all connected to a dead past, the memory of which swelled inside him like a cancer. It took genuine pain and sacrifice to change all this he knew—and that would be managed by names and faces. He knew that, too. He was again irrelevant as he had once been long ago.

A sharp draft joined him as he entered Alma's Cafe. "Close

the door, Herman!" the coffee crowd chorused from the counter stools.

"Go to hell," he said, moving on to his booth at the rear of the cafe. "When's the bus due, Alma?"

"Expecting somebody?"

"President of the railroad," he grumbled.

"Coffee?"

"Brandy."

"One coffee coming up."

He took his coffee and then turned his attention to the faces. They were old and familiar faces like his own. They were mourning faces, gathering not to spend money but to gossip and worry and compare, to warm one another with anxious chatter and to huddle against the prospect of doom. In a railroad town, doom is always the opposite of prosperity. Prosperity is seasonal and glowing until the fall of the year when ice and snow begin to close the season and dormancy sets in, and a long winter eventually leads to the anticipation of another spring, to the wagering and counting of days and the gambling of who will be called back to work and when. He had endured many such seasons and he was now so obsessed, he failed to hear the bus arrive.

A single person entered the cafe. A young girl. While heads in the booths looked up, the heads at the counter turned and boldly devoured her as she moved to the rear of the cafe. No more than seventeen, she wore her coat open with a scarf strung loosely about her neck. Her hair was light and bouncy as though she had prepared herself to appear casual, her eyes, staring blankly at the far wall, seeing nothing and everything. Had she been a cat, she would have leapt to the farthest booth to hide herself, but as it was, her veiled contempt for those watching made her uncertain stride both defiant and wary.

Herman knew all this at a glance. She was disturbingly familiar too, as though something of himself were walking through that door sixty-five years ago. As he watched, he couldn't shake the notion of her likeness. Nor did her mannerisms provide any clues otherwise

When she settled into a booth, he came to stand over her. Boldly he lifted his Homburg, bowed, hooked his cane over the back of the booth, and slipped onto the seat opposite her. "I'm Herman," he said. Once, she cast her eyes suspiciously at him, only to look away and pretend he wasn't there. "I'm Herman," he said again.

"You a constable?"

"You expecting one?"

"No."

"Then I'm just an old man."

"My boyfriend will be here soon."

"Good."

"Waitress—!"

"What'll it be, young lady?" Alma asked.

Staring up, the girl was speechless. "Whatever she wants, Alma." Herman said.

"I—," the girl began, then looking from Herman to Alma and back again, she said, "A coke—I mean, coffee—maybe a donut—"

"Maybe a beef sandwich and a glass of milk."

"No."

"What would you like, Herman?"

He waggled his coffee cup. When Alma had gone away, he said, "She'll help you if you're frightened."

"I ain't frightened."

"Then what's your name?"

"I don't have to tell you that—I'm just passing through."

"Your boyfriend's coming—"

"He's in Taconite City. I'm going to meet him. We're getting married."

"You're too young to get married."

"I ain't either."

"Well, some people are born older," he said.

"What does that mean?"

"Means you got instinct. I can tell that."

"You're crazy."

"I'll call you Mary."

"It ain't Mary."

"Beth, then."

She wrinkled her nose and grinned. "You're crazy."

"Now that you're Beth, where you gonna live, Beth?"

"My boyfriend—my husband will have a place."

"This is a fine town right here."

"He'd hafta go to work by bus every day—"

"A twenty-minute ride is nothing."

"Besides, we don't know nobody here."

"You know me."

"Hmm. I walk in here and sit down and some old man says I know him."

"Little kids and old people are always friends," he said.

"I ain't a little kid."

"Young folks," he corrected himself. "Old folks and young folks are just naturally friends."

"You talk funny, Mister—say, where is this place?"

"Baytown."

"Really!" she squealed. Instantly, she clamped her mouth shut and buried herself in the booth and glanced suspiciously about. "My dad comes from here," she whispered. "I got people here." Then she fell silent, thinking about it, trying to remember something. "No," she said at last. "He's dead by now."

"Who's dead?"

"I never seen him. I never knew him."

"Who?"

"A grandpa."

Herman grinned. "I'll be your grandpa. We're friends, aren't we?"

"You're really crazy, Mister," she said, clenching her teeth to contain a squeal and shaking her head in rejection of him. Herman nonetheless pursued an idea. "I got a little house. I'll rent it to you cheap."

"We can't live with you."

"I don't live there."

"You gotta house ain't nobody living in?"

"You bring your man here and I'll rent it free."

"Why would you do that?"

"Providence," he said.

"What's that mean?"

"Means you're damn lucky."

"Emery's funny about things," she replied thoughtfully.

"Emery—that's his name. Then the house is waiting for you and Emery."

"Oh," she exclaimed, glancing about. "I gotta catch my bus."

Anticipating her haste, Herman rose to his feet, clasped her hand and stuffed a bill in her palm. "A wedding present," he said.

"I can't take this," she said, glancing down. "Fifty dollars!"

"No strings."

"I might not ever be back," she whispered.

"You'll be back." And sensing her discomfort, Herman whispered as well. "You bring your man here. You can't beat free rent for starters."

"I don't understand—you're really crazy, Mister."

"I'm here every day at this time—just when the bus comes in. You bring your man. I'll wait for you. Right here."

"But—"

They had reached the bus then and that was the last he heard as she disappeared from his view. "You bring your man back here!" He shouted. "I'll give you the house free! The whole thing!

All of it! The yard and creek and garden and everything! The whole thing free! The whole damn thing!"

He stood waving his arms at the bus, the wind lifting his scarf about his shoulders. He cocked the Homburg comfortably over one eye and hoisted his cane in a salute to the departing girl. "Your man can sleep here," he whispered.

Then he started for the tiny house.

Business at Calahan's. Hak stepped to the edge of the walk and touched the shiny smooth hearse in front of the barber shop. It belonged to Calahan. Calahan was both barber and undertaker and attended both businesses in the same building, with his undertaker stuff stored ready in a dim room behind the barber shop.

The hearse was black. It was easily the length of two Chevy roadsters and hunkered at the curbside like a black cat. Hak liked the sweet smell of exhaust, the easy throb of the motor, and the spoked wheels that gleamed silvery in the sun. He trailed his hand along the body of the hearse to the rear corner where he saw people mirrored in the sleek blackness. On air they came, squat and fat, slipping away into space like balloons while the Avenue wiggled eastward toward the big lake. He couldn't see the big lake in his mirror, but he felt its cool breath sweep over him, teasing and colliding with the people on the Avenue.

He skipped to the street side of the hearse and again stared at his shiny black mirror as passing cars burst like flames, heatless explosions that made him squint his eyes. He could identify some and, for a moment he studied the flashing prints—a Studey, a Willys, old man Roscoe's Hupmobile and maybe Allison's Graham Page but none of them a hearse like Calahan's.

...And the Marine Bar. That reflected clearly in his mirror. It lay over the hearse like a stretched-out castle, bullying the Avenue, a credit only for its size. For his own reasons it was the enemy, and he closed his eyes on it now. Besides that, it dwarfed the Beacon Tavern a few doors beyond the Commercial State Bank. Cully was at the Beacon. He liked Cully. He threw drunks out the door and never allowed them to reach the flat overhead where he and his mother lived with the Man.

She was there now. She always was. He glanced up at the two slender windows fronting the flat. They gawked at the

Avenue without feeling and with shades drawn, they revealed nothing of the plain rooms behind them. From those windows Hak's mother got only a slit-eyed view of the Avenue, which she denied, but she always knew when he'd been to Calahan's.

The attraction there was not the barber shop. It was the parlor in the back, the assorted caskets and the smell of formaldehyde. Hak learned about these from Muffin who belonged to Calahan and who took Hak there when Calahan was out. She lived with her family in their flat over the barber shop and it was no problem for her to get into the funeral parlor below. Like now. She teased Nigger George to let them into the parlor, which he did, making a spooky face as he undid the latch, then he went back to his wicker chair in the barber shop and tucked his great hands under his thighs, his ripe eyes peeled for Calahan on the Avenue. In the darkness they giggled and when Muffin found the lamp on Calahan's desk, her shadow suddenly leered down on them from the ceiling and wall

"You scairt?" she asked.

"Naw. Lets us play undertaker," he said, leaping into a casket. "Close me up and I'll hold my breath 'til you think I'm dead."

"They look like that?"

"Like what?"

"A dead person—looks like that?"

Hak slid down on the velvet, clenched his fists hard at his sides and put on the solemn face of forever. Suddenly the parlor door flew open and Calahan stood monstrous in the shaft of light. "Muffin, goddammit! Git yer ass out of here!" Muffin shot behind another casket and worked her way into the darkness, while Hak crouched more deeply and held his breath. At the same time he felt tiny claws ticking over his ankle, and he knew he was in the company of ghosts. He was about to give up and cry out, but a cry not his own came out of the darkness. "Wheeeeee! Wheeeeee! EEEEEE!" It was a real ghost for sure, and Hak leaped from his hiding and raced toward the shaft of daylight and through the door to the barber shop. Muffin was already there, shivering and making a face and pointing a finger at the parlor door. Calahan was the last to emerge. He was grinning. "Dammit now, Muffin. You kids stay the hell out of the parlor." He flung one arm about her shoulder and dropped a coin into her blouse pocket. "Go find something else to do," he said.

On the Avenue Muffin said, "There is a real corpse in there, you know."

"There is?"

"Didn't ya hear it?"

"Naw," Hak lied and then raced across the Avenue to the rooms over the Beacon.

"Business at Calahan's," he announced as he strode into the kitchen. "The hearse is out front."

"You were playing in the parlor again?"

"The hearse," he said, interjecting the half truth.

"I'd as soon you didn't play there," his mother said. Without looking, Hak knew his mother stood planted in the mist of light before the sink, and he pressed the conversation.

"Somebody dead over there."

"Probably the disease of the Avenue," she said.

"Who, d'ya 'spose?"

"Cooney Martin, I'd guess."

"Who's that?"

"Nobody, really. Just a man. When I was a little girl—."

"You knew him then?"

She nodded.

"Where's the Man?" Hak asked about his father.

She didn't reply. But Hak knew. It was the reason he hated the Marine Bar and the reason he called his father the Man. It was a convenient disavowment of the man who brought misery to his mother. His voice deepened. "When you expect him?" She said nothing and he weighed that passive gesture against the sound of his voice crackling in his manly effort to face their situation. But always she clung to that little area about the sink, quiet, calm, monotonously absorbed, and when she did rise to the situation—

never directly on the subject, but skirting it with generalities of an annoying indifference—it was phrasing memorized and repeated to these rooms in the flat whether or not she had a listener. It was as though Hak was not there at all. He could shout that the roof was falling in and she'd say absently, "It won't hurt much." Or he could shout "Fire!" and she'd say with quiet assurance, "Run to the alley." But never did she face reality, never did she leave these rooms, never would she desert the flat.

She was a prisoner. He pitied her and at the same time felt a strange attachment—not to his mother, not to anyone he could define, say, like a friend who was loyal to a friendship—but like an object that he cherished. In her always-cotton-print dresses, snug over the gentle slopes of her body and cut neatly just below her knees, she was consistently pure and plain. Her hair glistened from brushing. It was cut square at her forehead and swept neatly over her ears to curl under at the back of her neck. It all seemed to pull her head upward in a permanent posture like the Indian head on a Pontiac car. But it had no purpose. She carried it like that for her own proud person who allowed nothing to be out of place. It wasn't even right to say she swept misery under the rug just to tidy up the flat. She wore misery instead on the whole of her person and it was fastened there in a kind of melancholy beauty.

Occasionally he'd say, "Yer pretty," and she'd smile, though it made her uneasy and she'd wrinkle her nose to dismiss the compliment. Nor did she ever look at him straight on. When she was serious she wore glasses, pushing them up on her nose and gazing over his head at something beyond. "Yer pretty," he'd say, trying to gain her attention.

"Hak—"

"Why don't you look at me?"

She shrugged, and her face became still again, trying to remember something.

Watching her confined to the sink in the kitchen, he thought about Mercy Calahan who was Muffin's older sister who bulged noticeably and who wore tight clothing that drew disturbing lines about herself. Mercy made him tingle inside, the smell of her perfume a sweet suffocation as her hand played on his cheek and her laughing eyes went long into him. She said "bugger" and "oh, screw" and chased after them when Muffin teased her about her boyfriends. "You little peckerheads!" she'd shout, increasing the mystery of her and making Hak want to be caught and feel her breasts against his back as her perfume swept over him. She was more than playful because it was always Hak that she went after and caught and squeezed, to his delight.

His mother, on the other hand, was sterile clean, odorless, and when rarely she held him against herself there was barely the detection of warm body through her cotton dress. "I love you," erupted from him, and then he'd laugh and say, "Pretty, pretty—I want you to be," thinking as he did, I want you to go out on the Avenue and fill yourself with people, smell apples and oranges and car exhaust or fish guts or the hot steel of ore cars as they grind onto the docks over the bay. At night she went to her room, and he to his, and they were then separate and alone in tidy rooms. But his darkness was full of color, oranges and reds floating across his sleepless vision—Mercy and Muffin and Nigger George and Calahan and all the Avenue which he could inventory as in the light of day. What was her darkness, though? Did the Man stand shouting at the foot of her bed, a tall and ranting ghost in the silk of night?

The Man was a shadow, his trousers bunched at his waist and heels and collapsed into pockets and ravines the length of his legs. From his waist up there was a gap until at the V of his shirt collar his Adam's apple bobbed like a cork when he swallowed or spoke. His image was as clear in the dark as it was in the daylight. Hak seldom saw him in daylight, but when he did, the man's white, hairless forearms hung from rolled-to-the-elbow shirt sleeves with huge, bony hands dangling at the ends like buckets. His face was sucked in and his cheek bones were high and fleshless. "He was beautiful once," Hak's mother told him. Still, the only fullness about him now was the black beard which hid pale gullies of flesh. "He's sick," she apologized. But this meant little to Hak, because when the man shaved it was only a few steps from there to the Marine Bar again, leaving the rank vapors of musk to linger after him.

And a day later, there was about him the smell of talcum that he used to hide the prickly stubble of beard. "Where you been?" he'd shout at Hak's mother as he came through the doorway. "I say, where?"

"In these rooms," she replied, softly defensive.

"Like hell. I was up here and you wasn't in!"

"I was here."

"You was somewheres."

She was silent, and the man could not stand silence. When he argued, he wanted opposition, he wanted her to fight back because her silence was accusing him. "Doc," he said. He pulled her from the sink, swung her about and eyed her, on his face now an ugly smirk. "Doc was up here and give you money, feelin' sorry for you and the boy—and maybe something else," he accused. Placing his great hands on her shoulders, he pressed her backward against the wall. Hands at her sides, Hak's mother stood calm as a statue, her eyes looking through the man into the distance. "Doc's a good friend, ain't he?"

"Edward gives me nothing," she said.

"Edward!" the man cried. "Friendly as hell, ain't we?" He pulled her out, and slammed her against the wall again, working her shoulders with those huge hands. Finally, in almost a friendly way, he grinned. "I know you ain't no lily. Hell, I've known all the time you ain't no lily." He released her shoulders then and backed away, his thumbs hooked in his belt as he weaved like a tall tree in the wind. Suddenly he began to whimper. "I know you ain't no lily." For a moment, her eyes focused on the man's face, then as though counting the buttons on his shirt, her eyes slipped downward to his waist. There she closed them, preparing herself. And a moment later he knocked her to the floor, half in the hallway and half in the kitchen, the neat hem of her cotton dress high on her thighs which swelled round and beautiful before Hak's own eyes.

He remembered the time she raced crying from the bedroom, her housecoat flying open, and he saw the delicate lines of her thighs flow into the darkness of her sleep-warm body. It was a shock, not so much that she ran out crying, but that she was exposed. He'd never seen her naked person before and his eyes fastened to the mystery of her and the mystery was exciting. She had suddenly become something different, not the quiet and stable woman who moved like a phantom about and around him, excluding him from the secret circle of her being, but raw and exposed and revealing everything about herself, crying and broken and naked in his presence. Another time the Man burst into the kitchen, drove at her, tore her dress away and pinned her against the wall while he pressed her breasts and stroked her bare stomach again and again, laughing and screeching with a weird sense of joy. She didn't cry out. She didn't run. She endured in silence until the Man dropped from exhaustion—and then she asked Hak to help her move him to the couch.

But seeing her that time before, sprawled on the floor, cowering, waiting for the ultimate humiliation, Hak was awakened to a new kind of affection for her—like the protection of a whipped and doomed animal.

"Don't you dare!" he had cried. He ran to her and fell face down over her exposed body and kicked and squirmed and yelled so the man could not strike her, generating an unexpected confusion that warned the man off. Hak ceased yelling then, and lay suspiciously still, waiting. Then he began to cry, pinching his eyes to forestall the tears, allowing at last a sense of relief and triumph to flow fully through him. At the same time he felt his mother's warmth and the strangeness of her body beneath him. He felt awkward and excited. Until now he had thought of her as beautiful and pure but she was something else to the touch, a something that made him think of Mercy Calahan, of her closeness and warmth that made him squirm with this same nameless delight.

He had rolled aside finally, and watched as she gained her feet and walked calmly to the bedroom, and moments later returned clad in another neat cotton print dress. She swept the floor and straightened chairs and went on to the pots and pans in the sink, her endless existence.

Restored, she seemed to have no memory of her humiliation.

"Why do you let him do that?"

"It's not me he hates," she said. Like all the times before and all the times to come, it was no more than a pinch wound that stung for a moment and was gone forever.

"Let's move away," he said.

"Where to?" she said.

There was gentle Nigger George, of course, and Muffin and Mercy and Calahan. "Muffin, goddammit!" Hak's father never spoke to him—even like that. In Hak's mind, he was just an object that pushed at the Man like the wind to find gaps in his clothing and chill his skin. Calahan was gruff, all right, but after a rage he'd put his arm about Muffin and, as though he didn't know it was happening, let a quarter slip into her shirt pocket.

Which made the Avenue a special place. "To the other end of the block," he said, risking little in the transaction. A beam of light drove through the window near the sink and restored the color of summer to his mother.

"You're growing up, Hak. You're thinking." She slipped sideways onto a chair at the table, crossed her legs and looked down at her hands folded on the oil cloth. Her hands were almost invisible with cleanliness. Mercy had smooth, oily hands that floated through the air and came to rest upon him like a bird. "Just this once look straight at me," he said.

She looked up and her eyes were clear and round. "I have something to tell you, I think." She dropped her eyes again, then pulled them upward to fasten at a point over Hak's head.

"Look at me," he said.

"Your grandfather owned this building, and when he died,

he gave it to me, and we've lived here free—and collect a little rent from Cully downstairs in the Beacon."

"Which grandfather?"

"Your father's father."

"Then I don't like him."

"You mustn't say that. He was a good man. He was a smart man. He gave this building to me in a will, excluding—" She paused, and again focused her eyes thoughtfully into the distance, "excluding the Man, as you call him." And falling back into her routine, her eyes never got back to him, but Hak began for the first time to understand. The flat was her castle. The only time the flat meant a thing to Hak, on the other hand, was when Doc Pavore visited. Then they all sat in the living room, his mother complete and smiling.

"Just waiting," Doc said. His cheeks reddened. "It could be no problem, Alice. I make that offer to you—well, for me, too," he said.

She glanced from Hak to Doc, wondering if Hak understood what Doc was saying. "I would do just what I'm doing, no matter," she said.

"I know. Some would think that's a tragedy—but that's not you, Alice—never pity. Stubborn, maybe. I gauge that you've simply attached yourself to an idea, a principle, and won't let go."

"I am old fashioned, Edward," she said. "You're right about that. It's an idea so deeply bred in me—"

"How you endure?" he asked gently.

Hak's mother did not reply, but there was warmth in her face as though she wanted to please Doc. Finally she said, "Until Cooney Martin comes." She laughed, but it was unconvincing. "It's just an expression," she said.

"You've said that before," Hak said.

"Who's Cooney Martin?" Doc asked.

"Nobody, really. My father's mysterious hired hand when we were kids, you know. If the cat's new litter disappeared, it was Cooney Martin did it. If a pig got sick, it was Cooney Martin did it.

Just anything bad that happened, it was Cooney Martin did it—a nobody who was always cleaning up life and making it rational." She paused and looked into the distance. "We kids believed in the mysterious Cooney Martin."

Doc rose and grinned, the lines deep in his cheeks. "You're so gentle and childlike, Alice. I don't wonder at you anymore. Your mother should have named you Pillar." Hak's mother rose, too. They stood close and almost touched, then Hak's mother pulled away. "I believe I envy you," Doc said. "—Take care of her, Hak." And Doc was out the door.

"He's a lot different than the Man," Hak said.

"Yes," his mother said. "But your father gave you a name." She did not elaborate. He knew she was not honoring the Man. She was saying instead, "You must understand. You are big now, Hak, and you are given this to accept." These rooms over the Beacon, the Avenue, the nights of dreadful anticipation, the steam heat, the stuffiness, the sound of heavy footsteps, her terrifying calmness and humility as she intercepted the Man with her calm and gentle defiance. These he must accept.

Suddenly the wall was between them again. He felt that. But he was different. He knew that, too. "You are big now, Hak. You must understand." And he did understand. She was his mother. And one thing more, she was a woman and with that revelation, he knew he would intercept the footsteps. From now on he would intercept the Man at the door.

But on this day the footsteps he heard belonged to Doc. His face was a mixture of gentleness and relief. Large and gentle he stood in the doorway like a cautious intruder. "I think Cooney Martin has arrived." he said.

"Yes, I know," she said.

"Does Hak know?"

She turned to face him and searched his eyes directly. "I've been trying to tell him," she said, reaching out and almost touching him before she retrieved her hand.

"Can I help with anything?"

"Calahan has—" She paused and studied Doc affectionately. "It's enough that you're here."

Doc wrinkled his face in a sorrowful grin. "Be sure to let me know what I can do then, Alice." And he was gone.

Hak's mother was back at her sink, her prison. Was that all she knew? "It's your father in Calahan's parlor," she said calmly. She was quiet again and seemed unchanged, and Hak stared at her back, waiting. At length she said, "I feel empty, Hak. I don't know what else to say—but we must show respect." Suddenly she broke from the sink and gathered him into her arms. "Sometimes we mourn for the wrong reasons—I mean—." She clipped her words and moved back, gripped his shoulders at arms' length, and for the moment looked deep into his eyes, trying to reach a part of him that would understand—"we're not always prepared—."

Hak drew himself up then. The news seemed not to disturb him, for he had never known his father, nor had he seen him as a part of their lives in the flat. He was almost as tall as his mother now, too. He studied her long and carefully, but the mystery of her only deepened.

Finally, he went to the window and looked out at the Avenue, wondering if he would ever see it as she had. People still passed forth and back on the walkway. There was the bank president, properly erect in his fine suit, striding toward the Moose Club for his daily drink. There was wobbly old Albert and his little dog Piffy, fresh from the Marine Bar, on their way to the New Life Cafe for soup and coffee, each to occupy a stool at the counter—stalked as usual by Constable Hill. In black leather jacket, black breeches with hard leather leggings and pistol at his hip, he would sooner or later find a reason to lock up the harmless pair for their own good. Hak chuckled. It was funny. It was like a serial movie, but it was a real and continuing event.

Cars rolled by as before and the wind at play lifted scraps of paper like fallen leaves to new places on the block, the lazy motion of the Avenue hiding its mysteries behind silent walls and closed doors. He thought about Calahan and Muffin and Mercy and Nigger George, as well, all of it his place, his family—and the sleek hearse crouched at the curb like a cat—waiting.

Coarse tarpaper covered what long ago had been intended to be the first floor of the house. Long ago, also, the first floor of the house had become the roof over the basement in which he now lived with his wife Mara. So long had it been this way that the storm shelter entrance, now like a decayed tooth, was an ancient intent of completion. Four steps led up to the brief landing, then there were the unmanageable steps downward into the basement quarters, while to the right of these was the space for a doorway to the first floor. It remained just that. A space that looked onto a barren plateau.

Denver stood anchored on the landing. Under one arm a package was pressed loosely against his body while that hand, splayed against the shelter casing, gave him support. The other arm flung about in lazy gestures as he mumbled to himself. Finally, he turned and, swaying at the edge of this precipice, he looked down upon his friend Dooley. "I ain't goin' back no more," he cried! "I ain't goin' back. To hell with the Beacon Tavern. To hell with Cully Yoohan. To hell with booze an' all that rotten stuff—you believe me, Dooley?"

Dooley made a face and turned back to his car. Having given Denver a ride home, his obligation had ended. It had in fact ended when Dooley himself went on the wagon some months ago. Still there was that residual commitment to an old drinking buddy, and he went to the alley and his old Buick, shaking his head in an effort to shed forever the sense of responsibility.

Twenty minutes later at Dominic's gas station, Dooley eyed Denver stilting his way across the street, his legs braced wide to keep himself upright. "Dooley!" Denver bawled, his awkward gait closing the distance to Dooley's car. "You goin' downtown?"

"Crissakes, I just dumped you at yer house—"

"The ole' lady!" Denver shouted. He held up the package,

and a moment later poked his grinning face in at Dooley seated behind the steering wheel. Saliva glistened on his yellowed teeth as the sweet stench of his breath escaped in a swarm. “Gotta fetch this to some Hester woman over on Fifth,” he said. “Gotta run this for Mara.”

“I ain’t ridin’ you nowheres,” Dooley said, eying Denver with mild scorn. “You dumb shit. When you die I’m goin’ to sell your brain for bran’ new ‘cuz it ain’t never been used.”

Denver jerked his head back and peered at Dooley through misty eyes. Drippings like icicles hung from his great nose, and he hauled himself upright and sniffed. “Hell, Dooley,” he said.

He turned then toward Dominic inside the gas station. Pausing to steady himself in the doorway, Denver quietly searched Dominic’s face for attitude. Finally, he said, “You got a dollar, Dom?”

“For what?”

“Round out some change I got,” he said, grinning widely, the misty waste from his eyes draining into the gullies of his cheeks.

“You already owe me money.”

Denver winced and shook his head, suddenly remembering. “Sure I do, Dom. Why, sure I do. Hell, Dom, I never left you with no bill of mine—”

“Look,” Dom said, cutting Denver short. “I’m broke, but if I had a dime, I’d give it to Mara.”

“That’s it!” Denver cried. “It’s Mara’s birthday, and I need a haircut. It’s for Mara.”

“Broke,” Dom replied.

Denver rocked himself about then and addressed the vacated driveway. “I guess you know, Dom, I pull for you. I send aaall kinds of people here for gas. I say to them, I say, ‘Dom, he’s a hard worker and honest, too. He’s a good guy, I always say.” Then he stilted away, wearing the grin that had long ago become his permanent defense against insult and humiliation, the package huddled in the bulk of his jacket.

Jesus God O' Mighty, he thought, a fella can't count on nothin' no more, not a ride from a friend, not a dollar even. He pulled the woolen stocking cap down over his ears and closed the red mackinaw about his shoulders. The wind had begun to sweep off the big lake and it had bite. A helluva thing ta have ta walk, he thought. A more warming thought was, Dave and Karen on the West Coast. In all his life he'd never hisself been out of Lake County, just to show what kids did these days. Or Sally in—hell's fire, he couldn't remember, but he snapped his fingers until he could say it—Winona. Married a preacher down there. Three kids. He felt better because he could remember Sally and the kids.

Slowing to a halt and swaying on his braced legs, he began counting on his fingers. Four of his kids he could remember well—five because the fifth one he'd kicked out of the house this morning, or some time appropriately recent—the fifth one, the oldest one, too, always taking change off his ma so he could shack up with that fat gal up at Big Noise Inn. He grinned masterfully. Sometimes a man had to be a sonabitch.

And Mara. God O Mighty what she'd done to keep body and soul together. She put the fear of God in the kids, for one thing. She was a good woman, a damned good woman. He was goin' ta tell her that, too. He started on again, trying desperately to draw a bead on the corner lamp post at the end of the block—if it'd stand still. Looking down at his foot steps made him dizzy—but hell's fire, sawing a board was the same thing. You didn't look where the saw was cutting, you looked to where it was goin'. And again he concentrated on the lamp post, the basement in which he lived drawing him forth now like a magnet.

Feeling the cold swarm at her back, Mara looked up from her chores at the kitchen sink when Denver shuffled through the door. She let her eyes sweep over him from his rumpled stocking cap down to his cracked leather shoes. Between those two points she registered nothing nor did she have much feeling about it, except for the cold that skewed around him into the kitchen. "Close the door," she reminded him quietly. Even then, the cold came toward her on hands and knees. Once more she looked at Denver to say something, but then, she thought, in forty years of marriage it had all been said or thought about, sorted and discarded, the most of it being their basement quarters which had never become a house, nor, for an assortment of reasons, a home. All else was a diversion from the real words, anyway.

That was only one of their differences. Denver needed the boys on the Avenue. It had always been the boys at the Beacon Tavern and the rusty slop that took their hard-earned dollars. It took shoes and dresses and trousers from little bodies too, little bodies he'd helped to create, eight in all, and thank God how in ever they'd made it away from here, and even now she doubted he could remember how many souls had suckled at her breasts. She'd been fully a woman then; there had been the hope of a future with family and love that flowered from the energies of their youth. Others had survived the hard times of their youth, but, even then, Denver's weakness was apparent and strangely less so as it hardened with age. It was his make, she had decided. Now, with all the children grown and gone, love was only a scent hidden deeply in musty quilting, among clothes and tiny shoes and leftover memories. But it had been there! Oh Merciful God, it had been! Sighing with resignation, she eyed the package cradled in his arm, Maud Hester's package, a package he'd carried all day, a simple errand that was now too complicated for him. "Your food's on the table," she said, turning back to her chores at the sink.

There was Mrs. Knute with her tightly laced corset defining her dark bulk as she hung over me. "Ya, ya. Sooo you brook the spade and can do no more woork—vat I do now?"

A single black hair sprouted from a mole on her chin. Her lips were pursed and questioning as her Nordic eyes poked at me. They were all the more intense because of the peppered brows that became a single thick line across her forehead. This forced my eyes downward to her bulky, old-woman legs which were bent and parted and pulling her soiled, cotton-print dress taut across her knees like a lap to sit upon. One fleshy arm that had long forgotten how to hang straight was cocked at her side, the whole of her an immense presence frozen in time before me. "Ya, ya. Sooo vat ve do now?"

"You're angry," I said.

"Ya, ya—but it goes."

"Then we dance," I said, grinning up at her. A second arm lay across her back, and suddenly whipping it around, she tempted me with a thick sugar cookie, her scolding lips still pursed in warning—until laughter blew them apart and her hands flew out in hopelessness. "Ya, ya ve dance!" she cried, scooping me up and waltzing about the kitchen, humming loudly a tune in my ear.

We were the new family on the block and this old country woman had befriended us from the beginning. In particular, she liked me because I cut her lawn and spaded her garden and pulled weeds—all those chores a boy does for a neighbor but neglects to do at home. To do so filled me with pride, or perhaps it was an immediate fondness I felt for this stern but jolly old woman who was teaching me that anger should be intense then quickly dismissed—and, of course, to dance.

This was during the Thirties. In those days, families from

grandparents down to Baby Sue gathered at the Finn Hop every Saturday night and danced to the urging sounds of Big Ole or Little Oscar's polka band. Along one wall, tables were heaped with foods from the pots and pans of "hardtime" folk who knew how to wring tasty dishes from lean cupboards and while some folks danced, others supped and shouted and pushed plump faces at one another, abandoned to the common joy. It was a raucous affair that today would be considered civil disobedience.

On these occasions, Mr. Knute, a slight, quiet man with a hair lip, clapped his hands and laughed as his Missus crushed me to her bosom and hummed her tunes in my ear as we whirled about in an ocean of sweat. My feet never touched the boards, but I caught the rhythms all the same and one day would do a mean polka with a more compatible partner.

Years pass, of course, and memories fall into a comfortable disorder, for again this grand old woman came into my life. Guiding her 1932 Model B Ford into my service station one day, she bounced onto the driveway and demanded attention. Plainly she had not aged. Grasping my hand, she pulled me to the rear of her car where she stooped in her corsetted fashion and pointed a stern finger at the drive axle. "There!" she cried. "Check that bump for grease. Knute and me is take trip!"

"Where you going?" I asked.

"Larsmont!" came the reply.

It matters little that Larsmont was scarcely two miles from town. It mattered little, because in her tiny world everything was of huge consequence, her will and posture constantly on the attack, her lips pursed and intimidating no matter what her mission. In such a way her days were crammed with details and unpolished honesty and her life was measured in moments, but her eyes were mocking and merry as though life were a delightful joke God played on her.

It is impossible, of course, to describe Mrs. Knute in full and appropriate detail, for she was an apparition, always a shocking experience, more a feeling, a bright and lifting spirit between crises. These many years later when I experience private moments of joy, she often reappears as a ghost, and I mumble to myself, "Ah, Mrs. Knute."

Doc put it like this: "The poor bastard died as he lived." This epitaph for Hemo was graceless but succinct.

The Very Reverend John Carlson could think of nothing in the realm of honesty to say, nor did he know much about the deceased and, since no relatives came forth to attend, the good Reverend simply said: "We commit this body to whence it came, and its soul we submit to God in heaven, He who judges all mankind. Amen."

Doc and Morrie agreed they were not in mourning, nor had they ever expressed the slightest feeling for Hemo, such as might express friendship or even a marginal closeness, a matter which now tugged at their hearts. And so together they commiserated. "And the sonofabitch owed me a twenty," Morrie remembered, biting his lip as he said so and, in view of the circumstance, decided that maybe he had no regrets.

"Damn, I'll miss him," Doc said, waxing philosophical. "Hemo was everyman."

With that, they left the cemetery, returned to the Avenue and the Marine Bar where they took a table far into the din and there, born of a new respect for Hemo which deepened with the evening, committed themselves to eulogy.

"Damned if he wasn't," Morrie agreed, though he was embarrassed to say so and shifted about on his chair until he was satisfied that the deceased deserved some compassion.

"Wasn't what—?" Doc asked.

"—What you said before—"

Momentarily Doc mused. "Oh, yes. You're right, Morrie. His body was his inventory."

"Inventory?" Morrie asked, sinking into a stupor of thought. Both men remembered that Hemo's wool shirts overflowed at the wrists and waist and the crotch of his heavy wool trousers, suspended from black braces, formed an awkward bridge between his thighs just above his knees, allowing the cuffs to sack loosely about his hard-toe clods. It made him appear deceptively short, for the mass of clothing concealed a wiry frame and a thousand abrasions that sculpted the flesh and, like his trunk, his face was equally an eruption. The upper lip was split with a single yellowed tooth braced in the arch and he wheezed, more so because his nose was squashed, a condition that forced a perpetual sneer. But against all this, his eyes were the contradiction. At times they seemed to plead from heavy brows and at other times, with a sense of joy, they were electric, charged like the spears of hair on his head—taken all together, an apparition made piece by piece with all the parts in constant rebellion. It was difficult to tell whether Hemo was happy or sad, and no one cared.

"I dropped three tens bettin' he'd die and he won't do it—won't git hisself kilt!" Archie Cole cried. "A phenomenon," Doc said. He was the knowledgeable observer. As a young man Doc had studied dentistry, had later opened a practice in a small town up the Shore and had then taken to drink. The affliction eventually reduced him and he removed to Baytown, took quarters at the Agate Bay Hotel and found employment on the railroad. He was a mite of a man with tiny hands and tiny arms and sunken cheeks reservoired with liver marks. He'd seen for himself that two hundred volts of electricity scarcely touched Hemo, nor did heat nor cold nor abrasion. "See?" he said as his pincerlike fingers pulled at the skin on the back of Hemo's hands. "Genuine boar hide. No feeling," he said. It delighted him to stretch the skin upward and watch it collapse like the cold skin of a plucked chicken. "Archie, my man—because of a foolhardy bet, you are indebted to Hemo for a pitcher of beer."

Hemo drank heartily. Aside from Doc's admiration there were wagers concerning his ability to withstand pain and in particular, to elude death and for a time, his invincibility was beyond question.

Early in life Hemo had been a fisherman on the North Shore of Lake Superior. In those days, in a small craft he fished deep water, overloaded his boat, and constantly risked being swamped by enormous swells that tossed him about like a cork. Braving winters as well, he threaded nets where the ice permitted, retrieved them and picked his catch bare-handed. At times, while his small craft pitched in a Nor'easter, he huddled low against palisades of ice, where he ate crusts of bread and sucked juice from fresh herring. Then he moved from the shelter and worked his nets until his exposed parts were a high crimson.

Already a legend, it is said that his nerve ends had retreated from pain.

The legend carried over when Hemo began a career on the railroad during WWII. Working as an ore puncher on the long and lighted docks that reached out into the bay, he wore nothing more than his wool shirt and trousers. Nor did he think it a special feat to shinny up the twenty-foot light poles to cling swaying in the wind while replacing light bulbs. A few experiences like this and Hemo's life became a roulette.

Undeniably, the sight of grizzled faces pitched upward in awe of him was like a slug of bar whisky burning his gut and igniting his hair. Soon he began riding down the chutes into the ship's hold on tons of iron ore, only to surface mangled and bleeding as he made his way out to receive cheers and coins and prodding to do more. Almost at once the stakes grew, and he began performing daily, cleverly working his way toward feats that were truly unbelievable—at last to the most daring feat of all.

One day, poised high over the bay, he dove into the icy water seventy feet below. Like a sword he broke the surface and drove downward to hard rock. A bit stunned, he groped for direction, recoiled and shot outward to ram headlong into an ancient cast iron anchor. Pushing away, he raked himself over the jagged concrete of the dock footings, scored his body on projecting rods of structural steel and struck the rusted sheet iron of a sunken hull.

Thrashing about then, everywhere torn from head to clods, he finally surfaced, pulled himself from the numbing water and lay over on his back on the pier. Feeling no pain, he was nonetheless exhausted and was unable to grin when the workmen sent up a wild cheer, unable to grin when they clambered down the ladder to swarm admiringly over him, unable to shed tears of joy when they jostled and caressed his mutilated body. Monies exchanged hands and losers scorned his daring and the fights broke out. Equally cheerless was the single man who, frozen to his perch of structural steel, vomited at what he had witnessed.

Eventually Hemo was snatched away to the warmth of the watchman's shack. On this occasion, now shivering from the chill, he thrived on the adoration, but could not tolerate their squeamish patronage when one among them called the company doctor. In the confusion, Hemo escaped to his little shack across the bay at Fisherman's Point, and there stayed in reclusive comfort until his mangled body mended as it always had.

Emerging some weeks later, he entered the Marine Bar to receive a hero's welcome. He was hoisted to shoulders and ported about. Doc's opening speech went on a full forty minutes while Hemo, on his feet again, drank lustily from buckets of beer. He laughed even as he was laughed at, even as abusive humor rained upon his ugliness. It mattered little that the patrons called him an aberration or leprous, at all of which he snorted through his various nasal passages and went on guzzling beer, while Doc, in scientific language, explained the puzzling enigma. Assured that Doc spoke on his behalf, Hemo roved about like a mongrel pup. Some embraced him. Some tried to lay over the spears of hair on his head. Others threw coins at his feet. And still others pricked his flesh with pocket knives or tugged at his baggy clothing—or ogled him with contemptuous speculation. Through it all, Hemo rose to a glorious peak, his inner self consummate with free beer and sandwiches and pickles in brine, and the heated pro-con debates that flourished on his behalf.

Days later, however, Hemo found the Marine Bar strangely hostile. He could not believe the silence. It was as though a curtain had come down between himself and the other patrons whose bodies seemed to move in a soundless vacuum. His quick eye saw Hyme remove the sandwiches and pickles and hard-boiled eggs to the back bar. Ignoring Hyme's actions, Hemo crossed to patrons at the bar, stopping from time to time, waiting for a face to come around and break the silence. Deeper in the saloon, ore jammers ceased their grumbling when Hemo approached. Pausing at one table or another, he expected a buck, a half dollar, a quarter or a free beer just as before. He slapped shoulders, praised good card hands and jostled patrons in friendship, reaping an encouraging response from none. Finally, standing amid the trackless audience, he shouted "Hey!" But just as a trout guzzles minnows, his voice was eclipsed by the silence.

Truly, Hemo's life had fallen into a slump, and this pain he could feel. At night in his tiny shack by the water he tossed and could not sleep. A strange prickling sensation rose up in him, one he had not felt before. He paced. He thrust his head between his knees to think. He urinated on the stoop behind his shack. He went to the rocky beach and waded into the cold water out over his head, and returned, coughing and spitting up the cold mucus of misery. Still, the prickly sensation persisted. By the time ice and snow had brought a close to the ore season, Hemo had been afflicted by neglect beyond endurance.

In desperation he turned his attention to the carshop, which operated unabated the year around. There the clamor of steel and bells and whistles and electric motors was sweet on his ears, a courtship of man and machine—and a new Hemo was born. He would perform the greatest feat of his entire career. Such a feat would surpass David's slaying of the giant or Christ's walking on water and would, he told the gathering audience, take more guts than most of them had just to watch.

Instantly, all work ceased. Excitement grew and bets were

laid. For an intense moment, Hemo viewed the grizzled faces as a commander reviews his troops, then he turned away and singled out a giant air press. As he did, the prickling sensation that had plagued him for weeks began to abate. It pleased him. It pleased him even more when he pushed a clenched fist toward the plunging air ram and the spectators groaned. "Bets are laid!" A voice prodded him over protests.

At this single urging, Hemo pressed on. Calmly he laid himself on the smooth steel bed, stretched one leg out and began edging it toward the reciprocating ram. "More, more!" some cried. "It's gotta draw blood!" others cried. "Pull back! Pull back, you fool!" Hemo played the suspense, edging the leg closer and closer, heedless of the warnings and glorying in the shouts of approval. With each stroke of the ram, the steel bed trembled. Viciously it recoiled and struck, each time closing the gap on Hemo's leg. Eying the terrifying machine, Hemo was without fear right to that moment—that instant when the six-inch, glossy ram, smooth with oil, bit through his trouser into the flesh of his thigh, severed a tendon, killed a network of nerves and rendered Hemo roll-eyed senseless.

When he awakened he was in the locker room with the doctor bent over him. "You damned reptile!" the doctor shouted. "You're nuts. This leg is now forever useless. You might have killed yourself—from shock, if you're too damned insensitive to die otherwise. Don't you give a damn?" The doctor waved away an imaginary protest. "You're a consummate masochist, is what you are." Suddenly he grinned. "And besides that, it was an accident, huh!"

True to the doctor's prediction, not one witness described the facts during the insurance investigation. Those who bet and lost and those who bet and won saw the event as a horrible, unavoidable accident, nor could the doctor's suspicions contradict their collective voice. The ruling, therefore, provided Hemo with a substantial settlement and a monthly pension to commence on his forty-ninth birthday. The ruling was more than fair, but the sudden wealth made Hemo uncomfortably self-sustaining

After weeks of healing, Hemo emerged from his shack by the water and made his way across town. Pivoting now on the one petrified heel, he swung his good leg in a gracious arc, moving himself forward like a run-down toy. Still, the discomfort of his awkward movements gradually gave way to a subtle, more powerful anticipation as he approached the Marine Bar. Halting at the door, he looked up and down the Avenue, just looking at first, and then the prickly feeling swept through him again. It was nameless and he could find no relief from it, even as he pulled open the door to join his admiring followers.

Inside it was like a windless summer day on the big lake. He searched the booths along one wall, the card tables planted in disorder about the saloon, the pool tables and the patrons bent over them with cue sticks held rigidly in hands. He eyed the sandwiches and brine pickles at the end of the bar and Hyme standing like a statue on the lath grating behind them, his back reflecting from the long mirror behind the picket of whisky bottles, reflecting as well the bodies hunched over the bar, their meaty hands cupped lovingly about schooners of beer. Broad backs. Times had changed. It was in the air all about him.

"What the hell," Archie Cole said when Hemo singled him for a loan. "You got all the money you need."

"Just a lousy buck," Hemo pleaded.

"Ain't got it," Archie said. "You're a old race horse now," he added, laughing and looking to others for support.

Cranking away, Hemo ran his hand along the glossy mahogany of the bar and glimpsed sour-faced Hyme in the mirror. Then he turned his attention to Doc at the far end of the bar. Doc wore his white suit and white fedora and a neat bow tie about his twig-like neck. Doc always positioned himself near the street entrance as a hedge against his habit. "Apparently, I degrade myself to talk to you," he said.

"Chrissakes," Hemo replied, wheezing and sneering at the reproach.

"There isn't an inch of flesh on you worth examining," Doc said, supporting his position on the matter. "Not a man in here will ever again trust your invincibility."

"What'd I do?" Hemo asked.

Doc paused to think about it. "You were in that limbo between life and death where weaker men seek their immortality," he said. "For a while believers and nonbelievers alike felt secure—in a word," Doc added, "you loosed a sacred talent and provided the patrons with their favorite pastime."

"What'n hell'd I do?"

"You came under the scalpel, that's what. You broke the spell. It appears your divine endowment was a hoax." Doc turned away.

Hemo hung his head in shame. "I ain't never said I was special," he said, raising his saddened and hopeful eyes. "I need a buck."

"I'm bound by the fraternal order of ne'er-do-wells," Doc replied. Feeling no malice, he nonetheless could not be ruled by sympathy in this lofty matter.

"Hyme!" Hemo shouted, moving down the bar to throw up his palm. "A lousy buck, for chrissakes."

It is a mistake to regard Hyme as a mere bartender, for when he arrived in town he correctly reasoned that to operate a profitable business one must be Scandinavian. Directly, he became Scandinavian, and he adopted the language to perfection. In reply to Hemo, he said, "Vell—." It was a transitory expression. "You is lucky man, buck is all you need." He considered it thoughtfully. "Tousand bucks I need."

"Chrissakes, Hyme—"

"A buck what you ain't got is same as tousand bucks you ain't got."

Hemo pressed on. "Ain't I brought you business. Ain't I

been the biggest man in town?"

"Yah," Hyme agreed. "You been the biggest—but," he threw up his hands in despair, "one times a hunnert is a tousand what I need."

Throughout the tavern Hemo plodded, giving patrons the opportunity to make him a small loan, based not on his past greatness, but on friendship alone. "Pals you ain't got," Kaznopopelli sang out. "Is only audience you got."

At last, having racked up one hundred per cent disapproval of himself, Hemo shouted, "Hemo's buying!" And stepping to the bar and clearing a place for himself, he swung his arm in a great arc to include everyone. "Draw 'em, Hyme."

Hyme calmly braced himself at the bar. "You got money?"

"Like Kazno tells me—'make a check'."

"Better you pay cash," Hyme insisted.

"Sonofabitch!" Hemo cried. "I can buy this joint—"

"Cash," Hyme said. "Fifteen tousand I take."

In a flurry of thumps on the hardwood floor, Hemo pitched out the front entrance on his way to the Commercial State Bank next door. In about a half hour, he returned and swung up to confront Hyme, strewing bills along the bar. "Is fifteen tousand what you ain't got!" he cried.

Slowly at first, methodically, Hyme began adding up the bills. Little by little his enthusiasm grew, and then, finally, he expressed downright disbelief. Grinning slightly now, his composure did not betray the oversight of a thousand extra dollars. He merely nodded approval. He then produced the keys to the tavern, and with little formality, he loosed his bar apron, handed it to Hemo, sampled his own pickles in brine and departed. Neither did Hyme plan a trip to the South Seas, for he knew that within weeks he would return for the keys and reclaim his coveted post behind the bar.

"The joint's mine," Hemo sang out, and in spite of his wheezing everyone heard, "I'm buying!"

Days and nights and days thereafter they came, and the beer flowed like water over the banks of the Stewart River during the spring floods. They came; they drank; they remembered. Doc was on hand to tweak Hemo's flesh. Morrie took a stool next to Doc and declared what a great time he was having. Archie Cole bragged about his betting profits at the peak of Hemo's career, the empty mugs marching beneath the opened tap in an endless and foamy procession.

But one day the tap and Hemo's bank account went dry. He knew nothing about supply and demand nor profit and loss, but at the brink of a new disaster, Hemo was resourceful. He gathered together kegs and crocks and bottles and caps, all pending a home brew operation and, with the eager help of an amateur beermeister, the brewing got underway.

For some, brewing beer is an art. It requires the proper ingredients, temperature and patience. Hemo had no patience and no concept of detail and, having sought advice from an amateur, he received the genuine likeness in quality. Had he thought about it, he would have known that his clients were not concerned with quality. What did cross his mind was his sense of instinct—for the most part of his life he'd had a contract with good luck.

But then, owing to a few missed payments, the city shut off his electric service. Not the least discouraged however, Hemo merely packed his operation from the cool cellar up to the anteroom at the rear of the saloon under an immense skylight, where, in collaboration with the sun, fermentation was accelerated. Before long he was ready for his second opening and, on that day, he charged happily onto the Avenue and shouted the news. It was rewarding and he was happy, and with great industry he rolled bunged kegs down the steps to the cool cellar for attachment to the coil—now much less cool than needed for dispensing good beer. Nonetheless, Hemo labored on.

It was a warm keg that got him. Returning to the anteroom at the rear of the saloon, he wrestled a final keg from under the sun roof for delivery to the cellar. It exploded, and Hemo died from aluminum shrapnel lodged in his heart.

Doc and Morrie commiserated: "Poor bastard," Doc said. "Everyone wants to be somebody and Hemo had few assets—so he invented them."

Doc thought about it further. "You know, Morrie, we all thought of Hemo as a throwaway—."

Pause. Long pause.

"—I think he was the best among us."

Morrie said, "You hear what yer saying, Doc?"

Doc said, "Look around, Morrie, and see the company we keep."

Himself seventy-four and what had he ever been, what had he honest-to-God-worthwhile ever done? The question brought an uncomfortable wave of guilt in which he thought he heard Mildred's accusing voice. But it was not Mildred at all; it was the emphysema, the thick mucus in his throat, the green bile which he spat into the cuspidor beside his chair, closing his eyes to do it. "Blow up balloons! Mind the doctor!" Always the family scolded him because he used neither the balloons nor the oxygen. He felt no pain. "When you've all gone home," he'd say, with Mildred confirming what the family already knew; "He never does. He never does."

But the big question—he'd asked that of himself when he was forty and looked back at no accomplishment and again when he was sixty and saw nothing of value, and yet again when he was seventy-two and watched Mildred, who was sixty-two, frolic like a colt while his own enthusiasm was the humiliating comfort of no responsibility. Were there regrets? Had it all happened so soon and where was the mark of his years?

He rose from the recliner, stood weaving a moment, then started his journey through the house. Slowly passing from the living room to the dining room, he paused at Mildred's desk, the center of family logistics, excluding him these days, then on to the hutch cabinet to see himself mirrored in the polished glass panes of the hutch doors. Mounted like clouded gems in sharp edges of bone were two eyes, not his own, staring at a skeleton surely not himself, the skeleton bent like a whip with long meatless arms cocked in the habit of unremembered readiness. Topping it all were spears of fragile grey hair waiting for a hand to lay them over. The hand, the hands, he thought, bringing them palms up, were disgustingly soft for hands that had been cracked and callused and soiled for a lifetime, hands with the memory of a use that was out of style these days even if they could find the energy. Levering one upward, he made a feeble swipe at the hair, then moved on to the kitchen and leaned against the door frame. No pain. Just a condition that extended itself during Mildred's absence from home, an excuse to be angry with her for deserting him today, not so much that he needed her, but when she was out he damned well missed her!

On the other hand, it sometimes took the length of the house before he could appreciate her absence—he could explore, for gawdsakes! Sometimes he stole from the front porch and shuffled a few steps down the block, remembering from time to time to pull himself smartly upright, knowing that what his mind intended his body had long forgotten, knowing too, that his longing for the town was impulse and not reality. Like a fortress, the Presbyterian Church was anchored at the corner of the block, and beyond, the court house looked down on the Methodist Church dressed in white with a cross mounted over the entrance—all three monarchs defended by the WWI cannon mounted adjacent to the sidewalk in Tom Owens Park. He hadn't gone far enough to see that, but he knew it was there and, like himself, a symbol of something long gone. Too, he longed to see the oil house where he terminated an ore run and the YMCA where he showered off the coal soot, and the boys at Archie's garage on the Avenue; McCannel on his stool, elbowed over the counter, the wood bench with Brink and Potty Vold, and Dalhberg in a trench coat with a pair of new Red Wing shoes for sale, and Archie in his leather lounge reigning calmly serene. In the garage, good discussion always preempted business—until a real problem came along and Archie could apply his genius. Even then, the fan club followed along and the mastery of tools co-mingled with irrelevant discussion—how he missed those daily seminars. He chuckled. The Avenue had been the stuff of life and a valued source of misinformation. All gone now, remnants like himself, knowing as well that as he wheezed and pulled at air he could scarcely expel Mildred would appear shortly to reclaim him.

"Max, you're impossible," she'd scold. "You know you can't run off like this," pressure on his arm slight but firm, and even as he allowed her to face him about, "Leave me the hell alone!" he'd cry, defying not Mildred, but the illness. He could not tolerate weakness in others; he would not tolerate it in himself.

And later on the phone to Emmie, Mildred would report, "Your father's feeling better today. He's out on the town again," as though he just charged wantonly onto the street to call everyone foul names. He chuckled at the thought. It was Mildred's subtle and blameless defense of his behavior. It was how she tolerated him at times.

He just did things, is all. He exercised independence mainly to let his body out on its own or his mind, which at times emptied itself in disgust.

Still, how gratifying to have Mildred gone for the afternoon and not caging him in for his own good.

And so the kitchen. It smelled of things, of hot coffee and buns and pop-eyed eggs in a round of bacon. Or did he just imagine that? He had long ago given up smoking, even the pipe, which he had substituted for cigarettes and cigars and, since his meals were served on a tray before the recliner in the living room, the kitchen was mostly alien to him now. So were the basement and upstairs rooms—which were both impossible—the basement with the sterile smell of laundry detergents while the sweet aroma of lilac lingered after Mildred in the others. A little cigar smoke, he thought, would make the house more habitable.

Impulsively he pulled open the door to the back porch and stood gorging himself on the familiar. Here, lining the wainscot walls like shelves in a hardware store, were his cabinets and drawers of nuts and bolts and fishing tackle and the odds of a lifetime that made life worth living. His rifles hung from wood pegs, a saw and carpenter's square as well, and claw hammer and things he treasured but no longer used, and jackets and boots and coveralls with the smell of railroad on them. How that clung to his clothes and defied interment with the kind of sweetness that he appreciated just as an old dog appreciates rot. No retreat here, by gawd! The back porch was him, him as he'd been in the cab of a Mallet iron horse when he was young and vital!

Diesels herded the ore cars these days, he thought with disgust. It was a sign of the times. He chuckled now because he thought of the ties and steel rails that supported his old house—it was common fare in the old days, almost every old house in town claimed a piece of the railroad in its structure—and now all the old houses along the block were museums of those days gone just as the old Mallet stood as a monument on a piece of track down by the depot. He remembered pulling a hundred empties north to Allen Junction, to the Soudan and Ely for iron ore that smoked the rails on a return trip. Suddenly he felt like a romp. The outdoors called to him. The world needed him.

With great effort he willed his lungs to pull the smell of himself from the back porch and, defying for the moment the difficult reality of exhaling, he was in no hurry to release the satisfying aromas. Still, he felt a sadness, too. Upon his retirement, Mildred left everything in place where he could claim what he needed just as he had for years. Altering nothing, she remembered also to leave the porch a bit untidy, mocking him for all the years she had picked up after him and had restored it to a sort of careless order. He felt a sense of urgency, too, and grunted his approval. It made him feel—.

Suddenly and unconsciously his tongue rolled the slug of tobacco lodged between his lower lip and teeth. He'd not given that up. The cut plug had been a reasonable trade-off from cigars or pipe—another gift from Mildred and, again, her efficiency had preceded him and it was damned unsettling to have responsibility so completely lifted from him. "Dammit, Mildred," he whined in her absence. "I gotta do something worth while! I gotta do something for myself!"

Turning from the porch, he retreated through the kitchen to the dining room and on to the living room where he sank flat back onto his recliner, gulping air which crackled through his wind pipe, draining away the precious burst of life. There was no such thing as a deep breath anymore. In spite of his sometimes fierce laboring, air seeped in and trickled out with a mind of its own while he seemed to float in a room that swirled about him, each wall and each picture or painting as vivid to him as a still print, until he closed his eyes and the churning faltered to a halt. Even then remnants of the mottled vision lay behind his eyelids and distant memories flooded in upon him. Sometimes he—.

Carefully his leaden hands crawled over his waistline to converge at his belt buckle and there pressed downward on the envelope lodged beneath his belt, beneath his shirt, beneath the folds of his long underwear where it had ridden for many days now. The contents he had memorized and then had condensed to a single line "—the fifth party of the estate of Lewiston Maynard late of Sycamore, Illinois..." his father. His mind made only a vague connection, searching for what he had long ago dismissed. But his mother's death more recently, an equally tenuous connection, left an estate to be divided among heirs. Never had Max thought about an inheritance; never had he considered such a likelihood as an asset, nor had he known the value. Having moved to Northern Minnesota, lived a lifetime without that promise, he should have ignored the original inquiry, but the yield of a fortune was unbelievable and undeniably an intrigue. "What you want all that stuff for?" Mildred asked when he began picking up traces of his life. "Pulling things together," he replied, thus blunting her curiosity in spite of the excitement welling inside himself. "Life review," he grumbled, though he seldom looked at old photographs. But now Mildred hauled them out and memories gushed from the deep well of his forgotten youth. He was inspired and entered into a conspiracy with the mailman.

From that point on he took to the sun porch during that

time of day when the mail man would arrive. "Just being useful," he declared to satisfy Mildred's curiosity.

Weeks later the letter came. It was an officious brown envelope which required his signature of receipt.

"What's that?" Mildred asked.

"Nothing."

"What?"

"A surprise, Mildred. A secret. I do lots of funny things when you're out."

"I won't pry, Max, but secrets are only fun when they're shared."

"With you, no doubt." Mildred pursued it no further and the envelope had been stored under his belt. Now he drew the check from the envelope and held it at arm's length. He studied the ciphers of fifty-thousand dollars, studied also the scribbled signatures that made the check authentic—and felt nothing. It was unreal. Instead, he was amused by the irony which found him at this moment in the recliner with a check in his hand. "Lewiston, you old son-of-a-bitch." It was the final irony to his near-bastard existence.

"Your grandmother never liked me," Mildred once said to Emmie during a visit. "—Didn't like us, I should say." She paused, reflecting on the wonder of it. "She made a point of ignoring your father in her will. Thought I'd be careless with it," she laughed.

"Smart woman," Max said.

"Daddy!" Emmie cried. "When you're mad at me, you say I remind you of Grandmother. I thought you disliked her!"

"She was a bitch."

"Because you were illegitimate?"

"Who said?"

"Your stories are haunting you now, Daddy."

"I said I came early, is all."

"—So she never liked you?"

"Breast-fed her favorite—your uncle, Lewis. He never

left home, never married, never had family, never did nothing but clutch your grandmother's apron and, in the end, she favored him with everything." Max considered that for a moment. "Maybe he done that himself. Your grandmother had to be senile by then." He was convinced of it.

"So think if you'd stayed on the farm, Daddy."

"Couldn't stand it."

"You left the farm at 14 never to turn back—I know, I know. I've heard it all many times."

"Not quite," he said, and fell silent.

Within memory was the time he returned home to borrow money for a team of horses and Lewiston refused. And then a second time when he married Mildred and needed a down payment for a modest home. "I come penniless from Sweden," Lewiston said, his cold eyes leering at him over a bushy moustache and tight mouth. "—and done for myself." His posture was uncompromising, and Max never humbled himself again.

So complete was the break that over the years he never gave his parents another thought, never initiated contact for any reason, but instead established within himself a mental block which, to this day, had served him well. It was Mildred who made the overtures, Mildred who forgave and believed in family at whatever cost, and it was Mildred who reached out though communication which was often only one way. Were it not for Mildred's aging parents who came to live with them, his children would have been without grandparents and Max would have suffered no loss. To this day, he felt that in his gut. The reasons were clear. Lewiston's refusal to help long ago was understandable, but not forgivable was the horse whip handy on the barn wall, waxed and spiked there like a prize rifle, nor the coldness that hung between his father and mother and himself with the implication that he intruded upon their lives, nor the utter coldness that pervaded barnyard and house and infused dialogues with hate and suspicion, nor the spare leftover food when he came in from chores, nor the privileges granted his brother Lewis who did little to earn them. In the remote room in the attic of the Illinois-style clapboard building he either sweltered or froze. Loneliness was his companion and the eventual evil conviction that he was worthless. Most damning of all, he came to despise himself! Long into his manhood that feeling crowded him, suffocated him and anchored to his bones when he left the farm and no one cared.

It was Mildred, finally, who taught him to enjoy. Cautiously at first and against his will, against all he had experienced in relationships, he placed himself in her custody while she coaxed him a step at a time to accept—and finally to trust until at last he began to like himself. It had endured these years, but only within the tight circle of the family as it grew.

His boyhood experiences, nonetheless, continued to be an influence. In the upbringing of their children, placed mostly in Mildred's hands, his reversion was consistent. When he disciplined, as always by instinct, there came that moment when impulse reached back in time to a bawling voice and cruel hands that held a whip and, lifting his detached members to the side of a child's head, he caught himself, waiting for Mildred to intercede—and she always did. Caught in his confusion of love and hate, she placed herself at risk with his ancient anger. "Find out what this is all about and I'll deal with it later!" he'd cry, and race out to the garage and stand behind closed doors to face disapproval of himself.

His disciplining struck fear in his children. It hung over their collective heads just as the whip on the barn wall had hung over his. He had tried to be more temperate but always the impulse was rage and, even as the hand was poised to strike, he cried out for defeat, for the power of Mildred's presence to restrain him. When his anger abated he had wanted to say "I love," had murmured the words in his prison behind the garage door, had struggled to pull them out of himself, but the moment never came. It was an extreme counterpoint within himself, an extravagance that his tongue resisted, and so he had never said "I love." In their place came the silent forgiveness that the family understood. They gave where he could not and he had anguished over this failure.

The consequence was enduring and subtle. During his productive life he had not labored for success. He had no mission for wealth. His every day was the intractable pursuit of creature comforts for his family—an unconscious payback with, of course, something special for Mildred.

"The Virgin Islands—?"

"I've always wanted to visit there, Max."

"How about Canada, just a few miles north? We could build a cabin in the wilds, light a big fire and be by ourselves."

"Who'd build the cabin?"

"You would."

"And you—?"

"I'd be boss."

Canada was his joke and the Virgin Islands Mildred's dream, but it had always been beyond their means. Still, they did study maps and make plans as though the dream would come true.

On impulse now, he dug about in his billfold and separated from the scuffed leather fold two blanched one-hundred dollar bills, pressed there like butterfly wings between the pages of a book. Thirty years if a day, they rode molded to the leather and no one knew about them, not even Mildred who loved to calculate and let coins filter through her fingers, coins she then stored in a huge jar. Hers was less a secret, though he never examined the jar's contents. His bills were tamped to permanence like railroad ties, secure from all raids upon his private capital. "Can I have my allowance, Daddy?" A dime. A nickel. A quarter. "Have you earned it?" "Can I have the keys to the car?" "What for? And no, costs money to operate a car."

He chuckled. Sure as hell they'll pare that from his hide, too. You take your triumphs and defeats and all you've been and all the things folks think you've been and the bones of your soulless person to the grave—but not one Yankee dime.

It was just a step from that thought to the next. He felt drawn and quartered these days. Sammie, for example, removed most of the tools to his basement some blocks away. Max longed for them, though he carefully avoided saying so and had no intension of using them again. But it was the principle—old hats, old shoes, old tools were clearly a man's province to loan as he willed and not be burglarized by offspring who claimed premature ownership. Like Sally claiming the silverware, like Mitzy already eying the precious china and Ben, deep into his studies at college, already declaring ownership of the bound volumes of National Geographic—all of them speaking up in lieu of a more lucrative settlement upon his death. Damn. That was a fact. And now he was excluded from every reference to the house and car and garage and the hedge that held back the street—all of it Mildred's, himself stripped, dispossessed, a decaying thing that only the devil could want.

"And what about you, Mother?" Emmie asked, sighting the loneliness her mother would inherit.

Mildred's small voice, "You're so spread out, all of you."

"Jesus Christ! I ain't dead yet!" Max cried from the recliner, his thin legs wrapped against floor drafts.

"Daddy—I didn't mean—."

"You, Mildred, have a snot-nose daughter!" Emmie offended him only because he yet had his last sane act to commit and not because the subject was taboo. Mildred and he often discussed the obvious.

"Your biggest battle has always been with yourself, Max."

Recognizing the truth, he replied, "I was a bastard."

"But, Max—," Mildred sat huddled on the couch, her legs tucked under and herself musing from a position of mild contention. "We were so busy surviving we never had time to be storybook parents."

"Mildred." Max paused to be certain she listened. He

knew she was attempting to comfort him now, a matter of little consequence anymore. "There's damn little insurance for you when I pull the pin." Damn. Had Mitzy forgotten the money Mildred loaned her for that house? Mildred would need it now. "We've got a small pension. It'll do," Mildred went on. "House paid for, six kids through college—and all doing us proud." She pointed a finger of pride. "We did do that, Max," as though what they had always expected of the kids were an accomplishment.

"On grocery money," he added, deferring to Mildred's money jar.

"No matter. The kids thought we were rich."

"All kids think their parents are rich." College for the kids had been beyond their means, yet the house mortgaged as well as grocery money saved were a sacrifice without regret. But the kids should never know. There was no lesson in a gift. Jesus for pompous—but there was no lesson in that. He and Mildred had done it on their own and it would be a favor to the kids that they should do the same. Or to think they had.

"So many times you needed a new jacket or boots that you never got," Mildred continued and as she did, Max lost track of her words, emerging later with another thought.

"If you had a wish," he said. "What would you wish?"

"For you to get well—."

"No, no, no. A wish for yourself—."

"A new carpet, then—all through the house—with professionals to install it."

Max grunted. "What ever happened to that trip to the Virgin Islands?"

"Oh, we talked about that years ago—or a trip across Europe on bicycles—."

"On horseback," he said.

"We couldn't fly, though. I couldn't fly."

"A cruiser?"

"Tramp steamer," she corrected. "We decided on that long

ago." Whereafter she went for the atlas, into the game now, planning a trip they'd never take. "It's fun to plan like this."

"We seldom ever talk," he said, feeling now the strain of conversation, working his ribs to expel his breath.

"Well, what is there to talk about, other than children and house and unpaid bills?"

"—and dreams."

"The St. Lawrence," she said. "We'll go out by way of the St. Lawrence."

In silence Max watched Mildred, the atlas open on her lap, her fingers nimbly tracing the unlikely route of an impossible dream, himself no longer thinking about that. Instead he weighed the tenuous odds of existing much longer, feeling more than ever the strain of breathing. Jesus! "You got some of that green spray?" he asked quietly.

"Max!" Mildred started from the couch and in a moment was beside him. She directed the spray, then knelt eying him with a silence that roared in his ears as relief slowly came to him. "I'll not go shopping with Emmie tomorrow," she said.

"Yes. Oh yes. I need my snuff."

"It can wait."

"No." He scowled and no more was said. Mildred understood.

She'd soon return from her shopping trip with Emmie now. As usual, she'd lug in a bag full of groceries and a bag full of dime mystery novels she'd found at the Goodwill store—and his snuff. He longed for her now, for the smell of lilac that rose from her person and swept through the house—and touched her pillow, a pleasant memory of the days when he could climb the stairs to her room. He needed to talk more. He had things to tell her just now. "I have a surprise," he said out loud. He could scarcely wait. That he had not earned the fortune was of no consequence to him. Mildred had earned it, and that lifted the matter from his conscience. "A surprise, Mildred," and she'd say—he knew exactly,

"In forty-five years, Max, you haven't surprised me once."

Oh yes. Oh yes. Slowly he pulled the brown envelope from the folds of his long underwear and extracted the check, which he laced through his fingers. A pen. He needed a goddamned pen! He sat forward to lever his frail trunk to its feet. It was damned heavy. Up. Up. Up! The hutch! The desk a mile away! The goddamned desk, the goddamned......!

Before the fire we had the T-Model Ford. It was the only gas machine on the farm and served no purpose other than to please my mother who was still more than fond of her pair of mares and the carriage.

It took just minutes to buy the T-Model. Father crossed from the Commercial Bank to Helge Jackson's garage one day and said, "I'll take that one." He laid down the cash and turned to me. "Take this out to your ma and learn her to drive."

"But I don't know a dang thing about it," I said.

"Learn," he said, and strode away.

My father was a horseman and he was shameless in his dedication. I have seen him walk along dreaming about horses, imaginary reins in hand and his fists clenched high on his chest holding against the imaginary power of a well disciplined pair. I have seen him pause along the way to stroke a muscled mare while reciting the facts of good breeding to her, her ears erect and attentive to the dulcet tone of his voice. "Not by the ton, my beauty, but can you listen," he'd say, "—intelligent eyes, sharp ears—you get a mare can listen, she'll out-pull anything in the county—look at them shoulders." Then he'd pass slowly along the length of her, his hand slipping lovingly over her sleek neck and back and belly and down her rump, until at last he stood back at a quarter view to gauge her bulging thighs and how the whole symmetry of her fit a winner. "Not like that brainless thing you got," he'd say, drawing a comparison.

"You mean Tom?"

"Brainless," he'd say.

"But Tom—"

"I ain't talking to you."

"Nossir."

At any time any horse along the way was subject to such scrutiny. My father's mind was never idle. He'd get the notion like the itch, and when it came on him he wore his black high-lace boots, black trousers, a black preacher's coat, adding to this the distinction of the black derby he stored on the carved-wood skull perch in his special room. He wore this on no other occasion, and so I knew on that day what he was about, that same day he bought the T-Model and dispatched me to Waldo to show Mother.

On that day I became the messenger. My mother was a tall woman, board straight and brittle with rich gray hair pulled into a tight knot at the back of her head and with fierce eyes that sighted off the tip of her nose. When she saw the T-Model in the yard, she came onto the porch and, for long moments poised like royalty, thoughtfully considered the machine. Then slowly she approached and surrounded it with her disgust. "Well, this team he's buying cost him this time," she said. "Now scatter and go about your chores. We'll not see him for days."

She left us standing there, me as well as Sid and sister Sadie who had joined us for the inspection. Sadie wanted a ride in the car. "We'd best leave it rest 'til mother gets used to it," I said. I'd scarcely kept the thing on the road on the way out, for one thing and besides that, Mother usually gave her permission for a new thing to stay on the farm once she'd thought long enough for it to become her own idea. I suspect father knew this. I suspect his impulsiveness seldom carried the weight of guilt.

"S'pose Father's thinking modern?" Sadie asked.

"Not thinking at all," I said. "I've been after him forever about a tractor like they got over at Hanson's, but he can't hear."

"Mother could."

"She likes horses as much as he loves them. Only difference is, she figures them to work. He collects them."

By this time Sid was sitting in the T-Model, cranking the steering wheel from right to left and making a noise with his mouth, roaring about the barnyard as though he were Barney Oldfield at the Indianapolis 500. I, on the other hand, was already looking down the road.

On the sixth day I saw dust lift over the hill that sloped down to the barnyard. Soon a pair of blacks grew in size. They were huge. Ears alert, their heads were high and proud and bobbing in cadence to their gait as dust exploded about their driving hooves. I knew my father coaxed them from behind. His derby soon rose on the crest of the hill just as the blacks had, salted with the dust of the miles he'd come. Perched like a king on his throne and with reins in hand, my father pulled against the powerful brutes. "Mind, lookit them heads!" he shouted. "See them knees and quarters! 1800 pounds apiece and not twenty pounds between them!"

The commotion brought the rest of the family onto the porch. It seemed then that the blacks pumped harder and stepped out more, turning their heads toward my mother's solemn reception and tucking their chins in a kind of mockery that made them accomplice to my father's vanity. Twice around the windmill they marched, then swung down into the gully between the chicken coop and corral and back up onto the buggy trail, churning at last toward the barn.

"Well," my mother said, fanning the dust from her face, "there's that automobile—but he didn't do it for me."

"You wanted it."

"Yes, and before that a new rug and before that a new carriage and before that a new water pump—all of them convenient excuses. Do you realize how many teams he's bought he don't need?"

"He needs them, all right."

"For hisself, yes," she spat. She arched her brows and pitched her head and peered down on me accusingly. "Over at the Hanson place they got them lug-wheel things now."

"Not completely, they haven't—when that thing they got breaks down, he rents them a team."

"And has two more standing idle. My word, how many teams can you rein at a time? And what about Brainless?"

"Tom?"

"S'pose he's fit to stand next to them in a stall?"

It was true that Tom hadn't pulled a wagon in three months because he'd kick hell out of anything we paired him with. "Plain ignorance," my father had said. "The sign of a cull—spirit but not temper, you want."

"Perfection," Mother said after my thoughts.

"They'll work," I said.

"These won't. These are part of his collection. In a little bit Tom will give up his stall to the royalty, and they'll be curried and shined and bedded down in new straw and stand for days like brass monuments—and no one had better find fault."

"He loves horses—"

"Bosh. They are possessions. They are a show of his ego just like them expensive rifles he keeps in the closet at the barn and won't let you touch, and them glossy, ornamented bridles he fondles and dreams by like a boy."

"It's more than that, I think."

"Like what."

I had this strange feeling that my mother was a 19th century woman, actually proud of my father, that she actually approved his obsession with horses but hid these feelings behind her sternness for the same reason he was unable to control his obsession. She was, after all, a strong, intelligent woman who, for the most part, ruled this tiny empire with her cunning and who usually had her way. But with one foot rooted soundly in the past and the other timorously testing the future, she was confused.

"Maybe he's afraid," I said timidly.

"Will you admit that Tom is a hand-me-down because he's brainless?" With that, she snapped about and drove everyone else into the house.

I stayed behind to watch.

My father always spoke softly to his animals and they seemed to sense his authority, attentive but not spooked by the constant drone of his coaxing. Only when the drag pole was dropped from between them did they toss their great heads in a moment of recess, then they took precisely two steps forward from their draw bars to freeze mid-step with their powerful legs gracefully scissored in the deception of motion, and remained so until my father led them into the barn.

Soon I heard planks being slipped from their supports and clapped together in some new form. I heard the stamping puzzlement of horses tethered in mangers strange to them. I heard the snorts and whinnies of confused protest and the thump of massive flanks against manger boards. I knew when my father went for water and when he measured oats into the manger bins and when he climbed aloft to shuttle hay from the mow overhead. Soon he lit a coal oil lamp and his bulk began moving across the row of small windows, now swinging a beam, now hugging a bale of straw and another and another, now hunched over with his shadow heaped in the window glass as he moved. When I could no longer see his shadow, I knew he had come to the front of the barn to his private closet to fondle the silvery hardware of his show halters. I knew that his fingers, waxed from stroking horse hide, caressed the cold metal, a fist clenched at his chest, guiding the new pair in full dress with tasselled harnesses and knotted tails. I knew that in the dim light away from my mother's efficient mathematics he listened to squeaking stanchions or bellies heave or velvet muzzles flutter as a new mare, settling into comfort, relieved herself. I knew that he stood inhaling the aromas of dry pine boards and planks, of dry hay and oats, of sweaty horses and harness leather and steaming hay-knitted manure. And I knew that for those moments he was at peace with himself.

I knew also that when he finally started for the house and his bed not a contrary word would be uttered.

The fire was a thief in the night. While we slept, its nimble fingers reached for dry wood and began to devour it. Soon it was the sound of water rushing over a fall and spilling onto the rocks below. It crackled and flared and threw plumes of smoke across the windows. And then in that moment of awakening when all the senses grope, I heard someone shout, "Fire! Fire!"

In the country a fire is a nameless terror. It's a constant concern, for its progress is rapid. And once it gets started, you know that help is miles away and woolly with sleep. You react with no sense of feel or motion while a second sense simultaneously parades the horror through you. You race to the pump house where supplies are kept and, while someone begins pumping water, others line up buckets for the brigade. You know your efforts are hopeless, but you don't think about that because you become a mindless machine. My father was already at the barn, throwing open the large doors to the stall alleyway. "Blankets!" he shouted. Even though outbuildings had caught fire by now and barnyard commotion had became a wail of panic, my father's attention was riveted to the barn. With blankets in hand, he waded into the black smoke that had already curled into the lower part of the barn. All about him chunks of orange flames fell and new fires flared. Wall-eyed horses, their muscles bunched, reared against their halter ropes. Back and forth they went, blindly charging their mangers and gashing their chests and shoulders on the snubbing planks, which splintered under the strain. One mare circled dumbly and forced her way into a stall beside her partner. Jammed together like this, their combined weight snapped the planks on either side, and one mare fell into an adjoining stall with her forelegs snared in the maze of dislodged boards. She was beyond help, but I grabbed a sickle from a nearby stanchion and cut her partner's halter rope, allowing her the freedom to move back, but she froze on the only spot familiar to her. She whinnied and cried.

"Here! Here!" my father shouted. Farther down the alleyway he was trying to free the new blacks. He tore blankets from me and threw them into the stalls over their heads, but they were swelled so tightly with fear, it was impossible for him to squeeze by and cut their halter ropes. Instead, he found a board and rapped them smartly on the rumps, whereupon, they both moved backward toward the aisle, then charged forward against the tether boards which snapped like sticks under the force. Now they were deeper in the stalls and they stood there petrified.

"Get out! Get out!" my father yelled. The hay mow was caving in as well, and each flaming splinter of wood set new fires. In the last stall near the door, one horse, its hind quarters prancing in the aisle, reared against the halter rope, crying for its freedom, but I could not help.

Gasping for air, I dove to the ground and crawled away on hands and knees and rolled onto my side, voiceless and clutching at dirt. Surely my father would die in the barn with his horses. At that moment, a single horse leaped over me, snorted and galloped away. It was a single horse, because amid the barnyard confusion it was the only sound I could distinguish—until I heard the rifle shot, then another and another, and I perked up just as my father appeared in the doorway, choking and gasping for air, only to see him charge inside again to fire more shots. I could neither reach him to pull on him nor cry out to him. Instead, instinct drove me further from the heat, even though it seemed I wasn't moving away at all. I tugged at myself to follow after him, but I was fixed on the spot, gulping air for myself, and when I saw him emerge like a ghost a second time, I shouted, "It's coming down!" But he stood there, all the same, firing at sounds until the sounds were no more. Then he flung the rifle into the crumbling shambles and walked away.

The water in the creek was black and deep and flowing quietly. I sat staring at it, draining out of myself and clearing my mind of a nightmare. There are times when a person is too numb to feel; there are times when a person sits in a vast emptiness. I don't know how long I sat like this before I became aware of my father standing quietly beside me. "I found this rolling in the grass further down the creek," he said. It was Tom standing just back of my father, his head drooped as though it were a heavy load at the end of his neck. A stubble of rope hung from the halter and I could see it had been slashed clean. "Smartest horse on the whole damn place," my father said. "Mind, don't you ever call him brainless no more."

He slipped down on the grass beside me. "Cool," he said. "Gawd, it's cool." He rooted up tufts of grass and chewed on them, scanning the early morning and breathing deeply as though he'd just now caught his breath and the swelling of his lungs made him aware of himself. "You handle one of them tractor things like they got on the Hanson place?" he asked.

"Maybe," I said.

"Learn," he said.

After a bit he stood up to go. His face, leathered and gullied with memories, pitched down at me and he grunted one of those offhand grunts that precede something important. "You better learn me to handle that machine your ma's got up by the house." Then he climbed to the top of the knoll and looked back, his sad eyes scanning the peaceful morning.

When he finally turned away, I watched his black derby slip from sight over the knoll.

t's mid-July. Through our tree cover, brilliant sun drives at the deck where we visit. It's a day made for fishing or trudging the rocky slopes of Lake Superior's North Shore, neither of which we'll do.

He wears a baseball cap, the visor pulled to shade his eyes, a baseball cap which he explains is "my fishing cap." His stomach rises mountainously as he gathers air to push the words from his lips with a monotonous but engaging drawl. Now and then his eyes sparkle and a lavish grin spreads under the visor of his cap, the grin that always precedes some intelligent nonsense that his busy mind conjures for our daily discussions. I learn today that from the combined DNA of a prehistoric ostrich and serpent a dinosaur has been born, a brontosaurus, he calls it. He sucks air and laughs because he knows I don't believe this, but to pursue the idea, he nonetheless invites me to follow his parade of possibilities.

Possibilities. That's why his baseball cap is a fishing cap, for he has long since given up the possibility of active sports. Even the fishing is a vicarious event when friends take him out for the day, an event that feeds his hungry mind to make possible the impossible. Such events spark his imagination on this journey to the brontosaurus. I laugh with him because he eagerly shares his world with me, a world I cannot know, but can savor by bits that lively imagination.

"You ever kill a bear?" he drawls.

"I have no need to kill a bear," I say.

"I do," he says, slowly and painfully describing his need. "That'd–be–a–real–trophy."

"The only bear I ever wanted to kill had me up a tree," I laugh, "—and he was the boss all the way." He laughs, too, not at my cowardice, but at my inability to experience a reality so vivid in his imagination. Yes, he's killed that bear and tanned the hide and hung it on his wall, all in a matter of seconds, and the magnitude of that feat expands with his casual grin. Then silence as his mind deserts that subject for another.

"What would happen if we all disappeared from the earth?" he asks. "You s'pose in a million years we'd start over and some-one—"(he gasps) "—would ever know we'd been here?"

"Nature always wins," I say, "but archeologists continually find evidence of our earliest ancestors—"

"You mean like apes?"

"Well, nature makes a lot of mistakes. All it takes is a few misplaced molecules, and another form is born."

Grinning, he shakes his head at the absurdity. "Then, then how—how come there are still apes around?"

At the foot of his bed and off to one side, a huge aquarium blocks a window and his view of the street. More like a wall against outside intrusion, it seems not to bother him, for the aquarium is home to his collection of languid fish slipping through the water as though it were clear jello. The smaller of the species dart in and about rocks and aquatic flora, adding color and action to this peace-ful scene. I wonder though, at the contrast of a bear skin splayed on the wall behind his bed, the furry pelts on other walls, the in-verted forelegs of a deer cradling a rifle, and the mock, long-barrel twenty-two pistol lying on a bed stand. All of these suggest vio-lence, or at least the favored activities of a once macho young man, who now anticipates my thinking. "The big fish feed on the little ones," he says.

"And—"

"I buy more–more of them." Pause. "You know how a fish drinks water?"

"Osmosis," I reply.

"How-how did you know that?"

"Well, they're in water. They must be saturated."

"I mean—the word 'osmosis.'"

"I guessed."

This satisfies him for the moment. Then the conversation turns to the universal subject. "You ever go to-to the Saratoga to see the girls?"

"That's still around?"

"You ever go?"

I see the trap—do we have this in common? Am I one of the boys? Was I ever one of the boys? This is what men do; they hunt and they fondle girls. I laugh. "I used to—a long time ago."

"My cousin took-took me there once—and this girl kissed me." His stomach heaves with the growing excitement of the tale. He grins broadly but his face reflects laughter. "She-she wanted me to go in back with her and have our picture taken—"

"And did you?"

"Ten bucks," he grumbles. "Naw." That was a disappointment to him. She intended to make commerce out of his innocence, or perhaps his dream of romance and, even though his imagination bore the need, the price was too high. Sometimes, though, any contact will do—a night nurse who attends him, for example. Once she french-kissed him, a memory that he describes with shame.

"Why shame?"

"Wasn't that bad?"

"Maybe she needed to kiss you. Maybe she wanted to. Maybe she did it for the both of you," I say, trying to squelch his guilt. "Everyone needs a little touch now and then—a little skin, as they say."

He grins with a frown. "Even you?"

"Even me."

"She has a-a boyfriend."

"Maybe they had a spat and she's venting her frustration." I measure my words at this point, perhaps for him as well as for myself. "The world has enough guilt. There needn't be any in yours."And in such a fashion we explore.

Whenever I visit him his splendid mind combs through the debris of theory and possibility, through history and paleontology and oceanology and electronics and machines. Real or imagined there is no trifle adventure. "You ever ride a snowmobile?" His stomach heaves and deflates as haltingly he explains: "I rode one over a hun–hundred miles an hour one time."

And there it is—in his bright eyes and playful grin, and that self-effacing attitude, all regret buried in a huge imagination which, like a complex painting, only suggests his deeper secrets and private feelings. Outwardly he sustains himself with humor and curiosity and I, with respectful excitement, reconstruct a young man.

For ten of his thirty-one years now, this young man has lain immobile either upon a hospital bed or, on the occasion of his only activity, a motorized wheel chair best described as a motorized bed. I do not question him about his paralysis, nor, for that matter, do I notice it. Pity is not required. Required only is the sharing of the trip through his wondrous world. Now he stares at the ceiling. A long silence this time, and I know his mind has wandered off in search of something. It becomes a game of anticipation where my mind tries to find order amid a thousand possibilities, yet, I am never surprised. "When I go fishing," he says at last, flashing again that captivating grin, "I like to smoke a big cigar." His stomach gathers his whole person in a great and final mound of our visit this day, and I sense an ominous moment. "My dad," he drawls, pushing the words from his lips, his voice now sunk in the solid terrain of manhood, "doesn't like me to smoke a cigar—but I smoke one anyway." He pauses and focuses those merry eyes on me, and where I expect a lively but inaccurate tale of conflict, I hear instead a quiet sadness couched in mischievous defiance. "I—figure—I—gotta—live—a—little."

His victory. And suspecting that we have touched his only physical connection to reality, I am surrounded by a victory as well. He has let me in.

Ellie says get out of here. Go some place. Do some thing. I know the rest. I come in for coffee and she's still in her housecoat. I come in to get warm, and she's on the phone. More coffee, and she's doing a crossword. "You got time on your hands, Allen. I'm still employed," she says. "Go find a purpose."

If I knew what that was.

Even the morning paper is boring. I'm down to the want ads now, in which I see one or two things I can do. Only, I got this thing—I'm too old. I ain't bad looking, though, not too pale and wrinkled, which is how folks see you. Hell, I shave every day and use lotion so as I don't stink. Got this paunch, too, but only so much as a notch or two let out on my belt. Course, I wear glasses, if that's a problem, not them contacts they got nowadays. Horn rims. Makes me look grouchy and gets attention. But there was this guy once told me, "Be good to little kids and old people." So be good to me. Ha. Ha.

Anyways, this ad is for an Adult Day Care Center, it turns out. When I step inside them automatic doors, I gotta tell you I feel like a kid. People with long faces shuffle about, hugging themselves against the chill; other folks strain at the past, digging up old lies and seeing vividly what never was in the first place. I know that 'cuz I done it myself. And them ones playing cards and games again. They got hot tubs, though, and that machinery like treadwalks and bars and swimming, too. I will say one thing, though, everything is painted bright colors like a fun house, like a rainbow crossing a summer sky. It kinda lifts you and people hurry about like they know what they're doing.

This one nun, for instance, Sister Mary Ann, I find out. She asks, "Can I help you?"

"Your ad in the paper," I say.

"What can you do?"

"I'm handy with a mop. Good with a broom, too, and windows—"

"We have people for that." Her mouth snaps shut, like extra words might fall out.

"It's your ad."

"Do you know games?"

"Poker. I'm good at poker."

"We don't do poker."

"Light bulbs. Door latches—?"

"Excuse me. Marie!" she calls out to a lady hurrying by. "Trouble?"

"Freddy again. He struck the nurse and dashed his food to the patio!"

"I'll be right along," Sister says, and she spins away without another word.

I follow behind because Ellie's always closing me down like this and I hate them closed doors.

On the patio, Freddy's in a wheelchair and the sun's shining high noon, but his face is swollen with misery.

"Marie?"

"He always does this, Sister. Darn him! Generally I catch it, but today he's especially irritable. I wish I knew—"

I butt in.

"Hi, Freddy. Must be real crap, you throwing it away like this."

"Mr.—what's your name?" Sister asks.

"Allen," I say.

"Well, it's not crap, as you say. It's very good food."

"Freddy don't think so."

"Freddy's not always rational."

"I wouldn't be neither, sitting in a wheelchair all day."

"He has to, of course. He's not ambulatory, as you can see, and we all have to make the best of his situation."

"What's his problem—I mean, besides the obvious?"

"He's very angry. He doesn't talk to us—or won't—and I'm not certain he hears very well."

"He hears, all right. Look at them hands gripping the chair. He's mad as hell about something."

Suddenly she whips her head around. "Are you a doctor? What are you doing out here and why am I discussing Freddy with you?"

"I can make him eat, I bet."

"Mr. Allen—"

"Just Allen."

Her eyes blister as they sweep down the whole of me, then move upward, slowly taking me in like I'm some kind of statue, until at last they lock on my face. "I'll—take—that—bet, Mr. Allen."

"Just Allen," I say. I find a chair and sit down before Freddy. Suddenly I feel like I'm in a war zone. I can feel the heat. He has no neck and his head sits on his shoulders like a huge ball. His hair is an army of thistles that tug at his scalp and his thick, fleshy cheeks, his eyes set deep in the folds and the color of blue ice. It's no surprise to find him board straight, his meaty hands poised to catapult his angry bulk. I know he was once huge and powerful, like he was a foreman in a steel plant or logging camp. I watch those hands as I reach for a tray to place on my lap. "One hand of blackjack, Freddy," I say, pulling a deck from my pocket and shuffling as they hit the board. "You win, I eat this slop. I win, you eat it—"

"Does he hear you?" asks Sister.

"We got a deal, Freddy?"

I lay out the cards. No hits. Freddy doesn't bother to look. I don't bother to look neither. "A deal, Freddy?" He scarcely nods, still eying me coldly. "I'll be back," I say, getting up.

Walking away together, Sister says, "You cheated."

"I know."

"And it's not slop."

"Freddy feels like shit, Sister. You gotta talk to him like

that."

"I don't approve."

Silence as we walk the hallway, 'cept I hear my shoes clop on the tile and I feel awkward beside Sister as she plows ahead like a barge in bay water. "You told Freddy you'd be back," she says finally.

"Freddy's gotta get even," I say.

"Well—?" She halts and wags a hand at me. "Go back then."

Anyways, every day now I'm talking to him, kidding him, feeding him, and soon I'm stooling him. You learn these medical procedures quick so everyone else can stay the hell away from him. Every now and then Sister swings by, asks how's it going, and then disappears. But even when she's gone away I can feel her at my shoulder. Once she says, "You're teaching Freddy bad habits."

"Nothing he don't already know," I say. Gawd, how he likes poker. He's obsessed. Ever since I tricked him the first day, he's out to get me. Sometimes he wheels his chair at me and barks my shin, and then pardons himself with this sly innocence—a real gentleman, this Freddy. Once he spits at me and I slap him. "None of that shit, Freddy. I can take everything but that." He hears me, all right. He bows his head in shame and I know I'm just the bush the dog pisses on. "Happy" he don't know about. But then, he's confined to that damned wheelchair all day.

At home I tell Ellie, but she ain't interested. "At least you got something to do."

"You don't get it, do you? Nobody wants him and he ain't got no place to go. They're just waiting for him to croak and probably none more than Freddy hisself."

"He's got family—"

"Naw he ain't. Board-and-care is what he's got. It ain't gonna happen to me, I tell ya. Comes my time, Ellie, I'm going off to the woods like them Indians done."

"You ain't that brave, Allen."

I think about it, though—Freddy's misery, this urgency of whatever it is he's gotta do, or whatever the hell's so important to him. He's planning. Behind them foggy eyes is cunning. I know 'cuz I see a kind of joy in his eyes when he beats me at poker, like he's saying to me, "See who's in charge?"

"Don't be such a asshole, Freddy. You gonna cheat, do it with class," I tell him.

For distractions, I think of this new game. With a pad and pencil in my lap, I ask him questions like, "Who's our first President?"

He scribbles and pushes the pad back. "Come on!" it says. "O.K. When did Germany become a country?"

Scribble. "You believe in God?"

"I don't know. Never thought about it."

Scribble. "You believe?"

"Chrissakes, Freddy. I don't know. Maybe no."

He sends the pad flying. I suck a deep breath, retrieve the pad and pencil and hold them on my lap, eying him like a whipped dog. Maybe he wants to believe. Maybe he's gotta believe, but I tell him— "I had a son once—I ain't got him no more."

Scribble. "What happened?"

"Vietnam."

Scribble. Scribble. "Shit! Damn! Hell! This damn world is going to hell!"

"What about you, Freddy?"

Scribble. "Nobody."

I feel sad for both of us, but it was all a long time ago, I tell him. "Anyway, you got me, Freddy. You believe?"

Scribble. "My God has heart."

There is this one thing, though. Freddy's happier when we're out for a ride, I notice, so I wheel him around the campus a lot these days. Always he pumps his body and beats his fists on the armrests, trying to get up speed, which I do for him. Round and round we go and when we get back, he's flushed and still pumping the chair. I think he hates it more when I go home than when I'm here torturing him. I'd never believe this neither, that you know in advance there's something happening but you can't figure it, something mystical. But sure as hell— Freddy asking me, do I "believe?"

Anyways, against all the rules, we go for a wheelchair ride one day, down the footwalk, across the parking lot and down the road toward the street. Right away, Freddy's pumping his body like a piston and hammering his fists on the armrests with such excitement, I skid us to a halt and go around to face him. His milky eyes are lit and he's still rolling like I'm not there, like in a fantasy with the wind still driving at him and ringing tears out of him—and this awful glee I can almost hear. I gotta get him back, I know that. But him pumping his body and beating his fists starts the chair rolling beyond my reach. "Freddy, for chrissakes!" All at once he's going crazy down the grade toward the street, his hands flying like flags, at the same time him pounding and coaxing that chair, and me chasing behind. You know how it is running down hill? Pretty soon your feet are just flying out back of you, trying to keep up with your body, the wheelchair and Freddy and me all out of control in the time it takes to yell "shit!"

I'm a mile behind when the chair slams a tree and dumps Freddy cramped to the ground, rolling and rolling as though he's trying to go on forever, until the ditch halts and cradles him just short of the tarmac. He's on his side, pulled rigid like when he's in the chair, his face set in this delightful anguish with tears flushing his blown-up cheeks. I don't dare to move him. I put his head in my lap and rock him like a baby. "I'm dead, Freddy. I didn't mean for this to happen. Gawd, I feel awful."

"You guys all right?"

Two policemen stand over us.

"Sister called," one says.

"How'd she know?"

"Don't underestimate Sister, old man."

"Freddy needs a ambulance."

"One coming," they both say.

I feel awful. I could die. I can't face Sister when later she approaches me in the clinic. "That was irresponsible, Allen."

"It was murderous," I agree, tears brimming my eyes now. But I feel a kind of joy, too, and I can't help it. "You should of seen Freddy. He was grinning, the damned fool."

Frowning no less, Sister turns away. "You ought to know better," she says, surveying the street below, toying with the windowblind now, searching for a suitable reprimand. "I ought to be real angry with you—I am angry with you!"

"I mighta killed him," I reply timidly, at which she whips around.

"Now stop that. It was an accident and in spite of your carelessness, that's how it will go on the records."

For weeks now we been playing these games, Freddy and me, and I could never get him to smile. But he was this time. He was really enjoying.

When the doc comes out, I ask, "Can I see Freddy?"

"He's a brittle and tired old guy," the doc says, "but go ahead."

Freddy's face is frozen with this look he always gives me, his cheeks pale as two scoops of home-made ice cream. He taps on the bed clothes and right away I know what it is. Poker. He loves poker, like everything is a gamble. "You're too tired, Freddy. You gotta rest." He raps the covers again. "O.K," I say. "One hand. No cheating, neither. One shot fair and square, and we'll see who's boss around here."

I shuffle and deal slowly this time and aware of my honesty, he concentrates on the cards as they fall. Fact is, I don't look at the cards. I watch him instead, seeing a kind of happiness that make his cheeks glow and I'm not surprised when he throws a ace over a ten right off. How can you beat that? It takes less than a minute to shuffle and deal, and then I see this long grin bunching his flesh until his eyes close—just as his massive hands lay open on the blanket and the cards slip away.

And then I see this new Freddy, all the anger gone, at peace with himself. It's like he's saying, "I win," and I sit there waiting to hear him say it.

"He lived three months longer than expected, Allen," Sister intrudes softly.

"You got schedules up there?"

"No, no. But you gave him three wonderful months. You should know that. He wouldn't let anyone else near him."

"He did have this big wonderful grin," I say. And I feel this bond I can't explain, this exhilarating triumph—

"Allen," Sister says, almost whispering, "do you believe in grace?"

"I—I don't know, Sister."

"Well—will we see you at the Center in the morning?"

"I don't know."

In silence we stare at each other, each feeling something different, trying to share the sadness of loss.

"I believe what Freddy believed," I say at last, talking to myself. "I believe in dignity."

She stands in the doorway now, half turned toward the hall. "Sometimes professionals erect a wall between 'thee' and 'thou,'" she proclaims, "—it's called 'survival.'" Then, "Allen, there are lots of Freddies."

And I know I'll be there in the morning.

A continent is opened to habitation, the mail arrives, and history is made.

On this continent, the many Indian nations had long had their runners and drums and smoke signals when the fledgling industrial part of this country was introduced to mail-by-rail and the Pony Express helped open the West. About this same time the Arrowhead Country of Northern Minnesota, far more hostile, uncharted and less known, had perhaps the hardiest of all mail carriers—pioneers like Robert McLean, Louis Plante, the Wieland Brothers, and the Beargrease Boys, to name a few. The latter of these bore a name already familiar to settlers along Lake Superior's North Shore, for Beargrease senior was not only chief of an area tribe, but preceded as a mail carrier his legendary sons, and was himself a legend.

At the same time, the Arrowhead Country was fertile soil for heroes and legends. For example, not until 1854 and by the treaty at La Pointe on Madeline Island, was the area opened to white man, who thereafter scrambled in search of copper, silver and gold. But more than a century earlier ambitious "*coureurs de bois*" (illicit French fur traders) had already experienced the mysteries of the Athabascas, the Rockies and the Pacific Coast, and had already trailed the countless rivers and sloughs and lakes west and north of the great Lake Superior. A vital point of departure inland was the Grand Portage, a nine-mile trek skirting the hazardous falls on the Pigeon River. Thus, often following the ancient trails of animals and least resistance, these hardy men together with the indigenous peoples, gave early prominence to the northern waterways.

Yet, the Arrowhead Country began its modern life as a mere inset on maps of Minnesota. It was still a dark and mysterious corner of the state not properly surveyed until the "Depression 30's" when the federal government made it a legitimate part of the map of Minnesota. Nonetheless, as permanent habitation arrived, the mail got through. In those days, the mid 1800's and on, the mail carrier was everyone's hero. For most of the year he was that solitary link to the outside world. He carried not only mail, but also carried news about marriages, births and deaths, and the weather. He knew when the overland trails were open and when the ice on the lake was firm. He told about immigrants arriving and new settlements springing up along the way, how crops were doing and who had purchased a horse. He was the equivalent of the modern day radio, telephone or television. He was a revered oracle.

From such a setting comes the legend of John Beargrease, and though he is symbolic of many such men, whatever truths or rumors make the legend, countless reports support the stature of this man.

Not the typical Ojibwe as described in photos and diaries, John Beargrease was a tall, lean man with a determined stride and a bearing that suggested mixed blood, not alien to the region during the fur trade era of some 200 years. He was the eldest son of Chief Mokquabemmettee (Beargrease) who arrived in Beaver Bay shortly after the site was founded by the Wielands in 1856. Because the chief had many wives, John's maternal lineage is vague, but it is generally agreed that he was a metis, again not uncommon, but a spicy addition to the legend. Two other boys were born to the chief as well, Peter (Daybosh) and Joseph (Showegan), and while they too carried mail over the same course, less is known about them. On the other hand, records show that young John married Louise Wiscob who subsequently gave birth to five children, three girls and two boys. For a time the family lived in a wigwam on the shore of Lake Superior at the mouth of the Beaver River and there are records of warm exchanges between the family members and settlers. Beyond that, memories have deteriorated and possibly diaries are lost, but a monument in the Chippewa Cemetery just north of Beaver Bay townsite indicates that most of the family members are buried there. Most other reports regale John as a tough, determined and fearless mail carrier.

One first hand report (William Stein of Two Harbors) indicates that John's eyes bore an unyielding fierceness and that his comportment as a cunning loner was typical of the woodsman, but he could be merry if the grog were plentiful. More than once (departing from Two Harbors at Burlington Bay) he was poured into a row boat laden with mail and pointed toward the deep water of Lake Superior where he immediately became a professional.

Even sober, this is a daring man's journey, for the great lake is huge and unpredictable. There are winds and swells and waves that match the oceans of the world, and especially along the North Shore, there are huge spears of rock that alternately hide or surface as the water rolls over them. During the winter, John guided his dog sled along the ice just off shore, crossing the numerous bays to save time. But since the lake seldom freezes over, the momentum of waves in distant deep water causes instant breakups, which zip along with the speed of light and often find man, dogs and cargo separated from land on an ice flow or dunked in freezing water. At times the winter was mild and John rowed his boat until ice blocked his way, whereat he towed the boat over the ice to open water again. As one sees, excluding a relentless wind, the journey was a constant torture.

The alternative was the overland trail. No less perilous were the deep and forested ravines. There were countless streams and gorges and raging rivers as well. In some instances shallow water made them passable. Over others, logs were laid to provide, at best, a precarious footing. But again a winter freeze stilled these waters and made them passable—generally. Even then, deep snow often covered pockets of open water, or blizzards disguised land drops into which one sank. Other seasons produced hazards as well. Rain, hail, slippery clay that clung to one's boots, windfalls and thick underbrush constantly athwart the trail.

There were mosquitoes, black flies and ticks, to mention smaller annoyances, and the itch from a morning dew, which woodsmen knew well. It is little wonder that local newspapers were fascinated by their mail carriers, for they knew the obstacles of travel. Such items as the following appeared with regularity: "As mail carriers, those Beargrease Boys...are worldbeaters."

On the lighter side is a second account from the *Hovland Locals*: "No newspapers were received in the mail of last week...It has been suggested that the carriers at the west end of the route lubricate their 'wheels' with something more reliable." Indeed, fun was poked, but never criticism, for none enjoyed more prestige and respect than did the mail carriers.

"Mail by trail" was a common expression in those days, and perhaps less a threat to fearless John were the bear and moose and wolves that shared his days and nights. For this menace, a brace of rattling bells on the dogs' harnesses aggravated the sensitive ears of the greater beasts and, in particular, the hungry wolves that stalked the dogs. During infrequent stops, a crackling camp fire made a substantial barrier, but while on the run the dogs were indifferent, at rest they huddled near the fire. These incessant perils, and more, earned for the mail carrier the designation of "professional." Between dogs and man was a bond of respect, a dependency and certain expectations. The coaxing rhythms of John's voice assured the animals that he was there and, in response, they were eager to run. When snowbound, man and dogs shared food supplies and whatever comfort could be obtained—the law of dependency in the unpredictable wilderness.

Perhaps more pleasant respites were John's trips north to Ely with a stop point at Greenwood Lake. Here waited the luxury of a woman's warmth. She also looked after his trap lines and fur business during his absence as a mail carrier. As always on the trail, his supplies were snowshoes, toboggan, dog team, tobacco, rifle, knife, dried meats (possibly pemmican) and foodstuffs gathered along the way. In addition to comforting John, the woman replenished much of these supplies. It would seem by this that equal to his energy were his head for business and his ability to survive. An address delivered in Two Harbors in 1934, by Postmaster Dennis Dwan, further alludes to the qualities of our "faithful servant."

"Day or night, good weather or bad made no difference with John; he was sure to arrive sometime with the mail intact. He was known to travel day and night without food (and I was going to say without 'drink,' but will leave that out) and when he reached his journey's end with his faithful dog team they would all rest up for a short while and start on the return trip regardless of weather conditions. He and his dogs were known to be snowbound for days at a time, but they would finally come through tired, hungry and frostbitten. But nature's wild wintery blasts had no terrors for 'Faithful John.'"

Another example of high regard for the legendary John Beargrease, and even more poignant is the flavor of the times and the hazards and hardships and the importance of the succession of mail carriers along the North Shore during the first fifty years.

But times change. Coinciding with "faithful John's" mail carrying days were the increased habitation along the North Shore and the combined efforts of Cook and Lake Counties to widen the trail from Two Harbors to Grand Marais to Grand Portage and eventually, on to Pigeon River. They appropriated funds for bridges and assigned county labor to keep the trail free of windfalls and the overgrowth of brush, which was as profligate as the first grasses of spring. Taking advantage of these improvements, John had a steel land barge fabricated. This could carry at least a ton of cargo, whereupon, he sold his dogs and purchased a draft horse. This barge was suitable for travel over ice or land alike. As the precursor of future travel, however, the horse hastened John's retirement.

Recognizing the wave of the future, the counties redoubled their efforts to widen and roughly grade the trail to provide passage of other teams and a mode of transportation that shifted from dog sled to horseback eventually made way for sleighs and horse drawn carts. Soon after, a stage line appeared as a public transport, carrying passengers and mail to and from Duluth, by now a flourishing hub for the Northland. In addition, settlements along the way were numerous enough to provide comfortable breaks in what was once a journey of isolation. Moreover, the ships that regularly plied the waters between Duluth and Fort William and Port Arthur, Ont. (now Thunder Bay) became more available to the outcrop villages and while not as frequent, they too carried passengers and mail and cargo, generally anchoring off shore where designated small craft could approach to exchange goods and to accommodate the economic lifeline of commercial fishing. What remains, of course, is obvious—the advent of still better roads, trucks, buses and all manner of conveyance. This is another story.

In any event, there are no ballads to tell the tale. What we know comes from news articles, diaries and word-of-mouth accounts, many of them in the context of John Beargrease the mail carrier. Doubtless he was one of the more salty characters of that era, and demanded constant attention as a mail carrier, as expressed so often in the *Grand Marais Pioneer*: "Bear Grease, the renowned half-breed pilot of the North Shore..." Even after he was eclipsed by the inevitable fortunes of change, local papers recorded his comings and goings and for sometime hence he remained an item of news.

Before that, however, Katherine Kirby Jones made an ominous entry in her diary dated April 26, 1899.

"Mail came at 6 a.m. The last trip John Beargrease will make this spring."

Very likely that entry recorded John's last trip all together, for in that year he did yield to overwhelming competition. Moreover, the continuing accounts suggest that he commenced a brisk fur trade with area Ojibwe. It is agreed, nonetheless, his death in 1910 closed an era.

The significance of this, it seems, is that a bounty of ethnic peoples forced the emergence of the Arrowhead Country from the primitive toward the modern. All were hard, tough and enduring people who accepted with equanimity the raw land and waterways, and not least among these were those men like John Beargrease who connected the Arrowhead to the official map of Minnesota.

The following two stories are chapters from Don's next book, Granite, which details the early history of the Arrowhead Region as seen through the eyes of the deserted French *engagé* Henri Jacques Basteaux out from Montreal.

In 1670 King Charles II signed the charter that formed the Hudson's Bay Company in Prince Rupert's land, an area south and inland from Hudson's Bay and the James Bay in Canada. At the time, none realized the expanse of land being chartered, nor was there any realization of the enormous wealth in this vast domain. This did not lessen the importance of the Bay Post, for during the next century it was not only England's single base of trade with the Indians, but it was also the seat of government for the area.

Preceding the Bay traders the French had already begun trade with the Far Indians and had ventured inland not only to explore, but to commence a busy cultural assimilation. Among the original French traders were Chouart and Des Groseillier who made their claims for the King of France and who were later arrested in Montreal by the King's representatives for lack of authorization, charged as *coureur de bois*, or unlicensed. Beyond them there were any number of traders out of Montreal, some legitimate and others not. Almost none kept diaries to record their affairs. Still, by the time Canada was lost to the British in 1763, these French canoemen had established posts in the Rocky Mountains and evidence suggests they had seen the Pacific Ocean.

In any event, these capricious *Pedlars* were a large part of the early fur trade business, and the first Europeans in this North Country to meld into the forest cultures and to mix, cohabit with and marry among the indigenous peoples. Undeniably, these traders number among the first European ancestors of many present day North Country inhabitants.

Henri Jacques Basteaux, out from Montreal as an *engagé*, hired canoeman, in the service of a bourgeois pedlar in the mid-1760s, knew nothing of the history preceding him in this area. He was uneducated and devoted to his profession. Likely his experience was the experience of many and though his separation from the trade because of an infirmity inflicted upon him during a struggle with a bear serves as fiction, none of what follows precludes his role as an ANCESTOR.

Ontario and Minnesota's Arrowhead, late 18th century

"You will die, Little Rabbit!" they sang upon his sepa ration from the company. "You will eat squirrel and fish and roots of the bush, and your dung will freeze at your heels!" Their cries signalled they knew the forest was treacherous. "You will need a squaw, Little Rabbit, a she devil with the spirit of the wolf!" They sang and danced about him and mocked his game leg. "The wolf does not pity the Frenchman!"

Now four days inland from the big lake and alone, their merry warnings were still on him. They had not mentioned his encounter with the bear that summer past, for amid the merry-making there was sadness at his parting. Lightly he drew his hand over his forehead and down the one cheek, feeling the still tender marks of the near-fatal wounds, the nose half-bitten away and the one ear sheared by angry claws. These were now his eternal marks, but it was the gimpy leg near torn from his trunk that caused his termination as an *engagé*, and that was his sadness.

While Henri was not entirely unhappy about leaving the hard life, considering his infirmity, he was also practical, though he did complain to The Almighty that the pack which contained his worldly possessions was now far less than the weight of loneliness. Halting to massage his game leg from time to time, he felt another weight upon him too, a strange heaviness while cool gusts of wind relieved him of the pressing heat. This brought him around to his aching limb again, and he put the rum flask to his lips to dull the urge to travel on.

Looking about, he liked the ring of hills and the trail following the ridge, and the noisy river below, as it tumbled through the gorge, though its seething commerce was becoming obscured by a distant rumbling and a gathering sky. It was time to build a shelter, he thought, and he began to cut boughs to weave about the birch tree that stood just off the trail. He wove them as the Ojibwe had taught him and he lay cedar on the ground for his comfort too and, completing that, stood back to admire his home. Next he stuffed his supplies under cover, then he took a pipe and another rum for comfort, regretting that his supply of rum was low.

The storm was sudden and swift, rolling over and down from the ring of hills to the ridge where he stood. Lightning split the sky and a thundering darkness folded over the day. Already high on the slopes, giant pines tumbled silently while green saplings lay over like wisps of grass. Below these, stands of brittle tamarack snapped mid-trunk and a tide of rain began to wash over the spoils as though a powerful hand moved the storm downward toward him. In moments a wall of wind and rain drove at him, and he, like the saplings, buckled over and clutched at roots and muck as he dragged himself to his cover and threw his arms about the trunk of the birch tree and clung as a mewling child clings to its mother. Beneath him the ground heaved and fell as his struggling anchor rocked in the wind, riding him up and down as though he were weightless. It was a dizzying ride as all about him the forest's anguished cry closed on his meager shelter. Never before had he been so helpless, so insignificant. Finally, his senses deserting him, he felt nothing, and he pinched his eyes shut and waited for the world to end.

Sometimes chaos is humbled by silence, yet the chaos lingers in the mind. Henri was aware only that he felt the tingling again and that pain returned to his arms, and he felt the whole of his body pressed tightly against the tree. It no longer rocked. It stood and the pine boughs still clung to its trunk as well. For this he murmured thanks to The Almighty, and yet again when he made a hole in his covering and saw the silent carnage and found that a giant pine had fallen and spread its protective branches over his lean-to. This brought him humbly to his knees where, in proper fashion, he made a promise concerning his salvation.

When later he picked his way into the open, he became

aware of new smells and new sounds and the forest seemed already to be renewing itself.

Overhead a hawk screeched as it raked the forest. It closed a circle to rest on a limb not far from where Henri stood. "Beggar!" he called up to it. The hawk rose and circled leisurely as though planning maneuvers in the quiet quarters of the sky, then made a graceful sweep downward to study Henri standing axe in hand. It hopped to a lower limb, then one lower still, its black eyes peering downward, its bill cocked. "Worms!" Henri offered. Smaller birds trilled homeward from their refuge during the storm. "Worms!" he called up to them as well, but the forest was busy and paid little attention.

Except the hawk. It flew off again, only to circle back and hold its gain. Engaged in the competition now, Henri became curious and he advanced toward the hawk until he caught an odor rising out of the dampness. He sniffed, and concluded the hawk was an undiscerning scavenger. "Henri does not eat rot!" he cried. Promptly the hawk hopped to a lower limb at a defiant level of Henri's line of sight and, no longer able to keep its secret, pitched a covetous eye at the quarry. Henri, too, advanced to see what the hawk had seen. It was then he conceded that the hawk was a capable hunter. "Mon Dieu," he whispered, peering through the tangle of brush. "What have we here?"

There, pinned helpless to the earth by a giant windfall, its great head a soundless, yawning sentry, was a grey wolf. The ground at its hind quarters was churned blood-red while the claws on the front pads had pulled torturously outward to expose bits of white flesh. Seeing it pinned in death, Henri was saddened that the wolf had known such pain, but remembering his own fright, he was happy for it, too.

He was about to turn away and leave the wolf to the hawk when he saw a leg twitch. Quickly he dropped the axe and knelt to examine the great head. He thought the snout quivered a bit, and he laid a hand gently on the furry neck and felt the hide tremble.

Then again he touched the furry neck and he saw something in the eyes. Milky and staring as in death, their dim black centers reached into centuries of distrust and defiance and instead of resignation, Henri saw the will to live. He had trapped wolves, shot them and, yes, even feared them during those lonely nights on the trail when they hungered from the darkness. But now the power of those eyes was telling Henri something about himself, something he couldn't understand but that pulled at him until he decided against the hawk.

He cursed his game leg as he stomped hurriedly to the lean-to and, again as he chopped away the tangle of branches that closed on the entrance, then dove for the saw he had taken from the Grand Portage to close his credit with the Company. He had a mission now.

Back at the windfall he cut a block which he rolled under the butt of the tree. Then he picked a stout branch to trim and fashion as a lever, and laying it over a block, lifted the tree enough to allow another support. Trimming a length of the tree, he cut the remainder free and levered that cut for support which relieved the pressure from the body. "Bon," he whispered. "What a fine lodging."

Making his way then through the tangle to the river below, he returned with a canteen of water. "So, a little rum and water," he said playfully, dribbling moisture on the wolf's snout. He sprinkled more on the disgorged tongue and watched for signs of movement, telling himself, "The forest shall not have the wolf—my new friend." And to proceed with his promise, he swept the knife from his legging and went in search of food, which soon yielded a careless rabbit, and a moment later it toppled kicking to the ground with a knife lodged at its shoulder. "Henri makes a choice," he said.

To the river again. Often before he had passed on this river with his singing comrades in canoes laden with furs. Often, too, the river was swift and a low branch or an unexpected windfall swept a comrade into the swirl and, respectfully, paddles were raised and the sign of the cross, but never did the procession halt for mercy. Now the river raged within its banks, carrying debris from the storm, but the river was no longer a formidable passageway for him. Like the bear or moose or wolf, it was an inhabitant of the forest. "One of us," he laughed, selecting a stout branch to whittle and notch to spear fish for the wolf's snout. Then he squatted nearby and watched for hopeful signs.

Until the storm, he had been preoccupied with his journey, finding his place in the forest and erecting a lodge and, during this time, he knew that wary eyes, with their quiet cunning had marked his intrusion. From time to time he had peered into the green darkness, sensing that other eyes watched him as well, anxious eyes with curious intent, but only the mosquitoes declared themselves. The wolf, on the other hand, had a presence like a campfire or pine pitch or the touch of a hand, all of which contradicted his mixed feelings of pity and triumph. Indian legends he had heard long ago expressed a mystic respect for all animals of the forest. They had no fear of them. In particular he remembered the legend of the bear that offered its flesh as nourishment for the starving children of the First People and, from that time on all animals were keepers of The People. "Anishinabe," Henri said. "Gidinawe-maagini-naanig-igoog," he whispered, recalling hauntingly the chant of an old squaw. "We are all relatives," and from deeper still came a woeful voice: "You are lonely, Little Rabbit."

Pondering the fate of the wolf, he noticed a leg twitch, and a feeble flare of the snout. He waited and watched. And the breast. Scarcely at first, there seemed to be a rise and fall that was becoming a rhythm and the snout seemed to quiver and collapse. This excited Henri, and he rose and stood apart from the wolf, thinking of a name to call his new friend. "Monsieur!" he cried at last. "It shall be Monsieur!" He clapped his hands and repeated the name, and his ears liked it.

Days later Monsieur was breathing nicely and tried to drag

himself whining from his prison. His hind quarters were limp, but his forepaws clawed soil and roots until he lay panting with exhaustion. At such times Henri interrupted his labors to squat against a stump and visit. Laughing softly, he told of himself as an *engagé*, of his comrades on the trail, of winter treks into the mountains, and often, though it fell to heedless ears, he exaggerated tales of heroism. He reached into his youth in Montreal as well, which he vaguely remembered, for it seemed he had always been old, had always labored as an *engagé*, haunted by a distant time that now seemed irrelevant. "Did you not suckle the breast? Did you not seek the tit?" he asked Monsieur. Laughing, he speared a piece of meat with a stick and prodded the snout until it opened and received nourishment.

By now Monsieur was more alert, and when Henri approached, he growled softly, his eyes steady with warning. Henri retreated but was delighted that those eyes followed his moves with that ancient suspicion, even though, at times, he wished to reach out and pat Monsieur's head as he would a dog. But respecting instead the proud wildness of his friend, he launched a new campaign. Not only did he shout and laugh and tell stories from a greater distance, but he sang as well, making his voice a constant part of the surroundings so Monsieur would always know from which quarter he approached. "Aha! Ho!Ho! Monsieur needs Henri—" he said proudly, "—and Henri needs Monsieur."

But at first light one morning as he threw back the robe and gained his feet, he knew Monsieur was gone. He called out and searched, knowing as he did that Monsieur, like Henri, was now finding his home in the forest. He had hoped the old wolf would accept his hospitality, share his camp and be a comrade, hoped so fervently that he had assumed it would be so. But now an emptiness fell upon him and he stood peering into the darkness that concealed the forest's secrets. Finally, he turned his attention to his own shelter again. There was much to do to get ready for the winter, but before leaving the camp he went to the river, and soon returned to place a fish at Monsieur's den. He had no words for such an occasion, but neither would he feel betrayed by his loneliness.

The hawk owned the sky again, calling out as it soared over the trees. Less noisy creatures observed from obscurity, passing the message along in a thousand voices as he thrust one leg before the other, and the sun drove shadows from hiding, revealing to him the beauty of a woman. "The forest plays tricks," he said.

Venturing further from his new home than ever before, he came upon a clearing and he paused, knowing he would find berries lush in the sunlight. At the same time he caught the odor. He would never forget that odor. It was the smell of beast rolled in rot with the smell of dung baked on its hide. He halted and stiffened, sweeping the knife from his legging and weighing the axe in the other hand. Then he saw the cubs wrestling playfully in the deserted open. Henri knew at once where he stood and he wheeled to see the great head rise over the bushes. The sow bawled a warning to the cubs, the pair suddenly bounding toward her, toward him. Again she bawled and, catching her tone, the cubs pummeled each other in their turn about to scamper for safety. As she emerged from the bush, peering dimly at the intrusion, her great head swayed forth and back to catch the scent. When she located Henri, she lumbered into the open and reared to her haunches, sweeping her claws through the air like scythes.

He remembered the bear of a year ago. He remembered the power, the stink, and how its claws raked his flesh. He remembered the old squaw, too, she who ran off the bear, restrained the flow of blood and held him to the warmth of her body. The smell of her was still on him, the grease and pitch and campfire smoke, and the strong hands coaxing him to consciousness. He remembered. And he froze.

He thought to turn and run, but knowing that a sow is aggressive and formidable in defense of her cubs, he stood motionless, eying her, his body summoning courage in spite of himself. There was no old woman this time. He had to charge, sink his knife at her belly, rip upward —and let The Almighty decide his fate.

Upright and bawling, the sow started for him. He dropped the axe, clutched the knife with both hands, raised it over his head, and gave out a curdling yell!

At that moment, the sow dropped to the ground and whirled and struck out, whirled and struck. No longer a clumsy mass, she disappeared behind the bush where a battle raged as she fended off an elusive assailant. While she was occupied, Henri could have fled, but the assault on the sow was so sudden, so intense, so brief she was already bounding away to the forest.

Moments later at the edge of the clearing the mysterious assailant raised a proud head and sniffed the air, then disappeared into the bush.

"Monsieur! Monsieur!" Henri called weakly, but his voice was lost to a sudden siege of nerves, and wrapping himself in his arms, he dropped to the ground and rolled in the grass until the tingling and trembling subsided, and he could breathe again, sucking deeply the crisp, clean air of the forest. Finally, lying flat on his back and fully appreciating what had just happened, he began to laugh, his laughter ringing in the hills. "Berries! Ripe berries!" he cried. "Monsieur will forgive Henri—there was this distraction!"

Ta Mante

She stood at the foot of the slope below the Frenchman's lodging, unkempt and greasy from her days in the forest. She was squat and fat as an old woman should be. She told herself she was no longer a flower of spring with the sweet juices of youth, but she admitted to a concern for the Frenchman.

She knew the Frenchman. From cover of the forest she

had observed these many days, and now knew his history as well as he did. "Fool," she said to herself. "Of course you suckled at a mother's teats. Does a bear? Does an elk? Does a wolf?" She was satisfied that he had uttered a longing more than a memory and this fit well into her plans, for her time was short and the girl-woman Snowflower must have a place.

So far the Frenchman had done well, excepting his encounter with the bear at the berry bush. Save for the intrusion of the wolf, he would have been a feast. Ah, but Ta Mante had long ago concluded that men are unavoidably stupid—had they only the wits to mix mind and bravery in good proportion—but this one seemed familiar to her and, considering the details of his person, nature could not duplicate this in another. Thus, viewing him as he stood on the ridge by the camp fire, she took a proud stance and called up to him, "Frenchman with the marks of the bear!"

Startled, Henri spun about and looked down the slope toward the sound of the voice. He was not prepared for a visitor and he moved forward until he saw more clearly a figure. "And what beast of the forest calls?"

"Ta Mante stands here!"

"Aha, a fat old squaw Henri sees!" he cried, moving to see her better. "Ho, ho! And now Henri sees a sow bear—too old for cubs! Does the she bear come in honor?"

"Fish is on the wind!" she said.

"Old squaw of hunger!" he laughed, feeling easier about her intrusion now. "Come then!"

Starting up the slope, Ta Mante muttered to herself, "This one plays."

And watching her approach with the strides of a cow moose, Henri confided to himself, "The hills see one that is no fool."

As she pulled herself onto the plateau, her nostrils flared with her breathing and without ceremony, she squatted heavily at a precise distance from the camp fire. "Smoke goes up," she said with a grunt of exhaustion.

"Smoke goes east and west and north and south. It does not go up," Henri chuckled.

"The Frenchman stands," she said.

"Henri is no squaw. Henri stands," he said, then he took a sizzling fish from the green sapling crutch over the fire and gave it to the old squaw. A second fish in similar fashion he took for himself, and settled down with his back to the fire, facing the woman. "Smoke goes in circles," he said. "This is not east. This is not west. It is where Henri sits." Soon juices of the fish trickled down his chin.

"The fish comes from the marsh," she said.

"And how does the old sow know this?"

"The river is swift and the fish lean. The marsh is lazy and the fish fat."

"Ho, ho. But the fish is from the river."

"The Frenchman was at the river," she said. "The spear was at the marsh." Ta Mante sat solemn-faced with juices dripping from her lips. Now and then she parted them to catch a breath, holding her eyes on the Frenchman.

"Do not make fun of Henri," he said playfully, sweeping the knife from his legging. "Short days ago a bawling monster was at the end of this."

"And did it run to the forest?"

"Oui. Oui. Aha, aha! It did not like the smell of a Frenchman!"

Silence. The fire crackled and smoke rose, dipping to circle the Frenchman on its way upward. "And did a wolf taste the heels of the bear?"

Henri rose up, turned to the fire, and then back again to face the old squaw, his brows crouched menacingly over his eyes. "Oui. And when Henri shits," he growled, "how does he shit?"

"As a bear," she replied.

"And you—," he sputtered. "You are eyes in the forest?"

"You are the man of the bear."

"Oui! Oui!" he cried, "and the wolf did set at its heels!"

"A bear, a bear!" she shouted that he might hear over the sounds of his own voice. "A bear near the camp of the First People at the end of summer near the edge of snow!" She wavered not a bit as his eyes bore at her. "A bear with the claws of the eagle with the blood of the Frenchman on them!"

Slowly he regained his calm, and he sat back, unwilling to believe that the old squaw could know of that bear. He remembered the strong hands, but he could not remember a face. Surely it had been an angel and this old squaw could not be that. Thoughtfully he considered the miracle—a fire, the warmth and smell of a woman in a mist like a dream, and when he awoke he was safe in the camp of the Bear People. "Aha, aha," he said at last, "the Almighty intervened—and as you see, Henri lives."

Ta Mante grunted, then levered herself upright and started toward the unfinished cabane. "Frenchman," she called back to him. "Ta Mante labored—your Almighty watched." And with a slight gesture of her hands, she moved on and into the cabane.

Stunned, and if it were true, Henri had not expected the mysterious savior to find him. Unconsciously he was in search of such a woman, aware that it had been a woman, but surely it had been an angel, not a fat old squaw with seasons beyond counting. "Ah well," he mused. "The Almighty would have to mend His ways in such matters." Still, he liked her. She was direct and honest, in spite of her acid tongue, and she had warmth and merry eyes. It pleased him most that she was the first human he had seen in weeks. Ah, but the acid tongue. "A wolf saves Henri and goes off in the forest to live. A fat old squaw saves Henri and takes his cabane." He laughed. Oui. He liked her.

Presently she emerged from the cabane, and having surveyed his work, she swept by him, and without breaking her stride, snatched the axe from a stump and proceeded into the bush. "The snows do not wait," she said.

For days thereafter Ta Mante's energy exploded in the vicinity of the hills. She charged from the forest with bundles of wattape and cedar boughs. With her expert care these items began to take a variety of shapes. A mound of boughs in one corner made a soft bed to lay upon. Soon, too, the smell of cedar overwhelmed the smell of decaying bark and the fetid rot of forest soil.

Henri, meantime, marveled at her industry and found that his own pace quickened to match hers. During these days a verbal truce existed between them and Henri no longer questioned her methods. He, in the meantime, made a chair to sit upon, much to the old squaw's dislike, but which she allowed so long as he understood her method. "This," she said, slapping his buttock, "rests here," indicating the floor matting. "Oui, oui, of course, of course," he laughed. "And one day the old squaw will crouch and not get up." She grunted, and peace was maintained while he made table legs and bunks to sleep in and more chairs.

Manageable logs had been notched and fit into place with smaller ones, stringers cut and fit for the roof, sweeping down from the peak to shed water. Cracks in joints were calked with rot from the forest floor, with green twigs crammed in to tighten the fill and wood pegs driven in to further secure the materials.

As the project grew from a crude dwelling it became sacred to both. It was true that Henri had decided a woman would share his lodging, though her dimensions and character had not been a factor until the old squaw happened along. Still, it was more than an accident, perhaps the will of The Almighty, he thought. Neither did Ta Mante expend her energy for nothing. She too had a plan. And so it seemed that each labored for a different reason.

But one day, just as she had appeared, she was gone, and Henri felt an acute sense of loss; another piece of him had been torn away and he talked to Monsieur in the forest. He told the wolf that the old squaw had given up her claim on him and had gone back to her people. He added that the smell should improve now that she was gone and they should be happy, thus again establishing his sovereignty over the matter of the cabane.

Still, only in her absence did he venture into the cabane, and this he did as though it were a shrine, for neither had taken up quarters inside before this. Because of their combined labors it somehow seemed sacred, neither willing to break the spell of their industry, but now he looked about, pleased with her work as well as his own. He was about to sit upon one of his chairs when he noticed that certain of his possessions were missing from the wall pegs. Instantly he flew into a rage. "Thief!" he cried. "Thief! Thief!" And he charged out of the cabane and down the slope in the direction she had taken a day before. "Old sow!" he shouted. "You have taken Henri's belongings!" Tracking her was hopeless, he knew, but the gesture made him feel better, even though he could draw blood at the moment. And how did one explain this? His mind could not understand this extravagance, and still breathing hotly, he fell back on the slope and looked at the river. The old woman had swept into his life, gained his trust, and then moved on with the cunning of a wolverine. These days he had tolerated her, and now this. But as he cursed her, mumbling these charges, his anger waned, and he began to tally his losses —a tin kettle and a tin cup, and possibly more that he had overlooked. Also he tallied the gains, and glancing back at the project, he saw not a cabane, but a palace. Suddenly the humor of it caught him, and he began to laugh. "She is a fox, that one." He laughed and laughed, and the forest knew there was love in his heart.

Days later Ta Mante stood again at the foot of the slope below the Frenchman's cabane. At her age the leagues of travel were without mercy. She touched the pouches at her waist and those couched at her tired thighs, one that hung from her shoulder, and another, a considerable one that tugged at the tumpline about her forehead. These were necessary gifts for the Frenchman, not because she paid retribution, but because it was the way of her people. Now postured to balance her load, she refused to measure the slope, grunting instead at her discomfort. There was nothing to say to a situation that had no ears.

Standing on the ridge, Henri felt a presence, and he came forward to inspect the slope and saw her and his heart was gladdened. "Aha! Ho! Ho! The wolverine returns!" he cried. "Wait! Henri must hide his pots and pans!"

"Ta Mante stands here!" she hailed.

"The wolverine—my traps, my pots!" He hastened toward the cabane, then turned to the old woman, grinning broadly at her discomfort. "Wait! Wait!" he shouted. "Henri must spare the wolverine a misery! He will call Monsieur!"

Grunting, Ta Mante started forth. She had no time to play with the Frenchman, and dragging herself onto the plateau at last, she dropped in a heap near the camp fire. Gulping air, she sat quietly, looking down at the river. For a torturous three days now she had clung to the winding trail as it traced the journey of the swift river, as it skirted cliffs and tumbled into chasms, tolled her energy upgrade and downgrade and over and around boulders that the Great Spirit Itself could not move, and more than once she had begged to be as the eagle, not only to lift herself over all obstructions, but in conclusive appreciation of uncomplicated flight. When finally the Great Spirit summoned her, she would again petition for the grace of the eagle.

Meantime, she was aware of the Frenchman. The joy had deserted him and he stood eying her, his brow furrowed and his eyes tender. "The tongue is tired, Frenchman?"

"Oui." Gently he lifted the brace from her forehead. With equal care he lifted the remaining packs from her person and placed them in a way to support her, touching her shoulder until she had positioned herself comfortably. "Henri's back has the ache," he said.

Then he looked down the slope at the river which held the squaw's attention. "And what does the old sow see?" he asked, chiding her, but in a voice soft and respectful of her silence. "Henri sees nothing," he said. "Henri sees only the river anxious to go home."

Ta Mante sat quietly pondering her reply. At length she said, "Ta Mante has a vision."

"Oui. And what game does the old sow play?"

"The snows come," she said.

"Oui."

"The Frenchman has no blanket."

"Henri has the hot coals of the fire," he said.

"The fire has heat," she said, "not warmth."

"Oui. Oui. And not a fat squaw that cannot climb to the ridge."

"Ta Mante is of an age," she agreed

"Oui! Oui!" he cried and laughed, and the laughter brought him to his knees and he rolled over and down the slope onto his back, "—and this vision!" he called back to her, panting as he visored his eyes to scan the river, "—this vision is a fire on the river?"

The taunting did not disturb Ta Mante. She knew the truth of visions. They were not mysteries. Visions were the wishes of the mind which, after a time, were made to be so. One need only concentrate. Ta Mante need only tell herself she has no future, the First People have no future, the white man invades and the ways of her people change. Ta Mante need only tell herself she is concerned for the girl woman Snowflower. She will share the Frenchman's blanket and mother a new and different people. This lives in her mind just as the grace of the eagle. "Frenchman!" she called down to him. "A fawn runs in the forest!"

Snowflower

The ripening of the rice would call them away again, to the sugar bush next and that would signal the snows, and the loneliness that clutches at the heart until the next summer's ceremonies. She did not let her mind dwell on the snows. She had adjusted well, she thought, and liked her place among the First People, though Snowflower could not imagine what that place might be were it not for the Mother Person, Ta Mante. "You will be of service to Ta Mante and no other," she had said. "Min-ma-wah comes late to Ta Mante's seasons." And then she called her name as Snowflower.

Often Mother Person was gone for days into the forest and none questioned her absence, knowing that only good would come of this. Snowflower always felt a sense of loss when Mother Person was gone, but she did observe that the First People made few demands on her and treated her with respect, as though she were a great spirit in the body of a child, for all knew that Mother Person's spirit watched from their lodging and brought Snowflower to and from without event. Through Mother Person she learned about the First People as well as the French spoken by the traders who came inland for furs. One day there was a curious sign outside her lodging. When she awoke, she saw first a single cedar bough extending south and east from where she lay. Immediately she wondered at the miracle her eyes fell upon, for never before had she seen this bough in such a position. It could mean many things, but most surely this bough caught in lonely extrusion from the main body of the tree had a distinct meaning. Mother Person on that day received her inquiry with "Snowflower will one day travel south and east." No more was said.

Lately the Great Spirit has been painting the forest. Is it not time to travel? Must one consider the snows? The real sense of this lies beneath the surface of self just as remembrance of the winds are in the mind. Mother Person says the perfection of this season lives in the joy of the moment. To be curious injures the future. Still, she has already declared a wintering place and this season will not share the blanket of the great chief.

"Always the old sow carries something!" Henri shouted down to Ta Mante at the foot of the slope.

She looked up at him, expecting to see him glowering down

with laughter in his eyes. Always the Frenchman plays, but ah, what a pity that the Frenchman is as clear to her as a day in the sun.

"And what does the wolverine carry this time?" he called out. "Like a squirrel, this one, eh. She goes with something. She comes with something. She comes and goes, aha, but never just comes and goes." he laughed. "The traders could learn from this one!"

"Fool," Ta Mante muttered and, turning to Snowflower who stood quietly behind her, said, "Ta Mante will test the wolf's bite."

By now his voice was the sound of roaring water in her ears as each step upward became more difficult for her. Now and then her mouth snapped open to gulp air and she discovered aches in her body that had not been there before. Suddenly she slipped and rolled backward to the ground, grappling with one hand to sustain herself. At the same time she noticed that the roaring in her ears had ceased and, looking upward, she saw the Frenchman pummeling downhill toward her, his game leg favored by both hands and without a curse issuing from his lips. Reaching her, he dug his heels into the earth, scooped her up and levered them both upright with a grace. When they were steadied, he continued clutching her. "And so," he scolded, "Henri must tow the old sow to the ridge." Holding her tongue, Ta Mante moved with the quiet comfort of his assistance, while her mind said, "The jaw has clamped shut with nothing between the teeth."

On the plateau, Ta Mante caught her breath and sat quietly looking down at the river.

"The eagle is out there?" Henri asked.

"Ta Mante has no more seasons," she said.

"Then the lodging is for the old squaw—she will climb the slope no more." Feeling sympathy for her, he thought about her condition and felt uncomfortable about it and laughed. "Aha, the eagle will not come. The old sow would send it away."

Ta Mante grunted. The Frenchman had not yet guessed her mission. What did it matter that she should die? She was of an age and had spent her seasons as she wished. No, Ta Mante did not pity Ta Mante, nor would she deny the eagle. Instead, with speculation she eyed the Frenchman. "On the slope stands a fawn," she said.

"Oui. Henri sees—but there is no rope about her neck." He glanced down at the figure scarcely defined by the distance, but who carried on her person many pouches. "Gifts?" he asked.

"Snowflower stands there," she said.

"And this Snowflower comes with the wolverine who likes Henri's pots and pans?"

"Snowflower warms the Frenchman's blanket."

"Oui," he replied to the sound of her voice, then: "Ouiiii – and now Henri hears with the ears of a hawk!" He rose and squinted down at the new wolverine the old squaw called Snowflower. Slowly then he started his descent toward her, stepping as one who stalks prey, fixing his eyes upon her figure in spite of the jolt each step made on his body. Sensing that he was doing the old squaw's bidding, he did not halt until he stood before this creature. When his breathing had quieted he saw she was almost as tall as he, but indeed a fawn, not like the seasoned squaws he remembered at the fort in the summer who were more than a match for the Hivernants, but a little rabbit, a delicate little rabbit. He stared. The rabbit stared back. Not a flicker crossed her large, brown eyes, nor did her person seem to breath. Glistening black hair fell over her shoulders and on her face were no marks of the forest, but rather the smooth newness of a sapling, and her neck was the graceful neck of the fawn. The buckskin she wore flowed over her predictable slenderness as though she had yet to bloom and fill it, but in her hands splayed at her waist, clutching securely the pouches that cluttered her frame, he saw a strength that denied frailty.

Slowly his hand found his cheek and drew lightly over the mutilations. Until now he had worn his marks with pride, but her obvious purity made him aware and uneasy and he whipped around and ascended quickly to the plateau where pausing, he told the old squaw he was off to find a bird for the bellies.

As he charged into the forest, Ta Mante struggled to her feet. These days it was difficult getting up and down and her body said it was impossible to hurry after a man who had spent his years trotting tirelessly over rugged trails with packs on his back. No matter. She knew she would find him near the tree of his salvation, near the wolf's den.

"A squaw that can lift and can carry, a squaw with marks of the forest—not a child," he said.

"A sapling bends to the winds while great trees fall to the earth," she said.

"A child!" he cried.

"A woman," she replied. "A woman child. It is the way."

"The old squaw can lodge in the cabane, then, and take this Snowflower to her nursing tits—Henri will build another."

"When the snows come," she said, "two lodges are less comfort than one." Knowing the enemy was pride, Ta Mante pursued her mission. Had she not seen the Frenchman bring a fallen wolf to good health? Had she not seen him nurse other creatures of the forest? Would a moose calf out of a fallen cow go hungry, or a bear cub bawling in a tree? Would he say now that a fawn was not worthy? "The eagle comes, Frenchman."

"She will go to the portage. A wife there will raise her well—"

"To be traded like goods?"

"—Then to the children of your people."

"Snowflower is not of my people. She is the spirit of Ta Mante—she lives only as Ta Mante lives."

"Look! Look!" he shouted, wheeling about to face the old squaw. "Are the eyes so dim?"

Approaching the Frenchman, then, and gathering the attention of his eyes, she said, "Only the heart is blind." She moved to touch his cheek. "The Frenchman is ugly. An eagle has clawed rivers of blood in flesh that was once pure. The she bear has eaten the ear where the sound of the wind comes; the nose hides in the hair of the face—and the stink of the Frenchman is as the moose with dung on its hide in the heat of the season." She made a face of disgust, then with a single finger gently traced the marks of his destiny. "—But the Frenchman's heart is the sun spread over the forest." She paused, caught her breath in a long sigh, enabling her only to whisper, "If the heart will see, Frenchman, a single flower makes the forest a garden."

She was about to turn away when Henri flung his arms about her and held her fast. He buried his cheek in the mass of black hair and for long moments let the smell of woman find his nostrils. He was aware of the old squaw's age and the coming of the eagle and he was saddened, for her spirit was the spirit of life. In the weeks since she had come into his life he had learned from her; she had replaced to his person all that the forest had taken. Oui. "The old squaw stings like a bee and drips honey," he said. "Why does Henri bother?"

She broke free then and defying her seasons, bounded away almost as in her youth. "The Frenchman stinks as a moose!" she called back to him.

"Oui! Oui! And a sow bear pisses on his head!"

As the first timid snows of the season fell over the ring of hills, a raw, less gentle wind lay against the forest, drumming the last of the fall colors to the ground. To assure their comfort and survival, Henri, Ta Mante and Snowflower had already established a routine of chores. A first priority was firewood and great amounts were cut and split and stored along the inside perimeter of the walls of the cabane. There were stones to gather and fit and caulk as a fireplace took shape in one corner and as a crude chimney rose to vent a ritual fire which, when lighted, would burn continuously. Stores such as corn, rice, maple sugar, dried berries and pemmican, all offerings transported on Ta Mante's person during her many trips to the various camps of the Bear People, would now supplement fresh meat secured from the winter forest. Herbs and medicinal roots, sometimes randomly acquired during the warm seasons, became a priority as well. This was one of the few times that Ta Mante broke the silence of their collective labors to issue instructions or impart wisdom. Her silence was not unusual, for busy hands labored without instruction and gave the mind time to organize.

Wrapped in his robe the Frenchman now resided at the base of a great pine while Ta Mante and Snowflower occupied the cabane. Days and nights like this Ta Mante did not predict, nor did she approve, but she reasoned that time erodes vanity and that soon the Frenchman would yield to the cold.

Also, the three of them took their nourishment from the fresh kills turned on the spit outside the cabane. On these occasions smoke from the fire rose up and surrounded Henri in his restless struggle with indecision. He had never before lived in the continuing presence of women. His thoughts considered the change. This child-woman, Snowflower, a constant helping hand whether he needs her or not, says nothing. She is just there, moving as a shadow and doing the right things with annoying efficiency. That he might become fond of her is also annoying, for she seems already to be inside his person and driving him at will. "Henri is clumsy," he at last confided to Ta Mante.

"Time is the teacher," she replied.

Meanwhile, it is clear that Snowflower remain at the Frenchman's side, assisting, observing and waiting. Always Mother Person made the decisions in matters concerning Snowflower, and always Snowflower obeyed in the tradition of the First People, but now discomfort fed on humiliation, and finally she gathered the courage to assert herself. "The Frenchman has no tongue," she said. "Snowflower is at his side and stands in emptiness."

Ta Mante said nothing. During her own youth a young man would court in the proper circumstance of chaperones, and Ta Mante would accept or decline as a privilege. She could toy with a suitor, seem eager and then not, accept or reject at her own whim, not because she was in no hurry to mate, but because she was young proud, burning proud and full of herself, seeking the range of womanhood just as a new cub seeks independence. But what did one do in these times when customs from two different worlds met? Ta Mante knew well that youth in love is mostly physical, and that marriage is an experiment on the way to a relationship. She knew well that good relationships are sometimes accidental and take time, and that time was the problem.

Standing before the child Snowflower now, she stroked the gleaming strands of hair. She touched soft cheeks and studied the clear, innocent eyes. They were steady and sincere but not at peace. They were curious and searching but not at peace. Finally, Ta Mante let her old eyes wander jealously over the trim, hard body not yet blooming with child. This was not the youth Ta Mante remembered. This was an experiment, the reluctant future that reached outward to a new nation of people and, in the privacy of her thoughts failure was conceivable but no longer practical. Also, in the privacy of her thoughts, Ta Mante could guide her people toward a future but could make a decision for only one. "On the Frenchman are the marks of the forest," she said. Turning then, she looked out the cabane doorway as though the wisdom of centuries flowed into her person. "The Snowflower has no marks."

Large flakes of snow slipped lazily from the sky and were already covering Snowflower's moccasin prints. Wrapped in a robe, she carried nothing more than a piece of pemmican and a knife sheathed on the calf of her leg and, though she wandered in pursuit of a good path, her general direction was toward the ring of hills. They were high above the ridge and. because of their height, pulled at her in spite of the marsh she must cross to reach them. Their importance was measured by more than their distance, for the treacheries of the marsh were the water holes hidden in islands of weed still summer lush and thick enough to support her weight. Knowing a misstep could be fatal, she stopped along the way to shape a branch to serve as a feeler and as a support. From time to time she halted to listen as well, for certainly someone followed her. She could feel it. Yet, all she saw was the Frenchman's wolf, Monsieur. He peered at her from the bush and when she moved on, he moved on. When she stopped, he stopped. Soon she was stopping quite often to check their progress and, since the wolf always peered at her from the bush, she began to speak softly to her companion. She knew that her words were gibberish, but she assured herself that the Manito, the spirit of the wolf would understand.

Soon the land rose out of the marsh and, as she became more sure-footed, she hurried toward her rendezvous with the ring of hills. Her mission was now clear, and she pushed all else from her mind as she made preparations. Selecting branches from a fine cedar tree, she made a mat to lay upon, clearing first the snow from the base where she would lay. Then, advising her personal Manito of her intentions, she drew the knife from the sheath at her leg. The remainder of the ceremony was reduced to a quiet whimper as she slashed one cheek and then the other, drawing a river of blood from either side of her face. She dropped the knife and gathered snow into her hands to press against the wounds to slow the flow of blood, and as she debated her worthiness because of the new marks, she snuggled down in her robe and was soon asleep.

When she awakened she had no measure of the time she had slept, except that she awoke to the daylight of one of the Great Spirit's days, and now she must check the success of her mission. Reaching a hand to each cheek, she drew her finger tips lightly over the marks and followed the ugly ridges of dried blood as though they were the sacred gifts of the Great Spirit. She thought at first to wash the dried blood from her cheeks with snow, but quickly decided that the healing was in progress and must go undisturbed. At the same time, sitting up with the robe thrown back, she saw paw prints all about her tiny lodging, and then the rabbit laying lifeless at her feet. That was a wonder. What had she done during her sleep?

Slowly, she looked about to see if her companion were still in the bush as he had been during her trip to the hills. Soon she saw him peering as before, and the next sensation was the burning in her cheeks as she began to smile. For the first time in a very long time she wanted to laugh and she could not and, fighting the urge, she nodded and murmured "Miigwetch." For surely the Frenchman's wolf had served her breakfast.

Anishinabe:
Spelling varies, but general meaning is The First People. Language derives from the Algonquin group from the Northeastern States.

Cabane:
A small dwelling in the woods.

Grog:
A diluted rum.

Gidinawe-maagini-naanig-igoog:
"We are all relatives." A reference to nature and all natural inhabitants.

Homburg:
A felt hat with stiff curled brim and a creased crown. Fashionable first in Germany.

Hostler:
A helper who climbed aboard and switched rail engines to various shops in preparation for the next ore run.

Hoghead:
An affectionate slang for an operating engineer.

Malacca:
A mottled cane made from Asiatic rattan palm.

Miiwetch:
A Chippewa term approximating "Thank You."

Mallet:

(Pronounced mal'-ley) With sixteen drive wheels, among the largest steam engines in the world, its maximum power was never fully realized due to limitations of roadbed and other restrictions. The last were produced around 1941, at which time diesel engines arrived on the scene.

Stutz-Bearcat
Packard
Willysknight
Essex
Studebaker
Hupmobile
Graham Paige
Model T:

Popular autos of the 1920's, 30's and 40's. A lapse in production during the WWII years reduced these models to relics.

To order additional copies of
Keeper of the Town
or receive a copy of the complete
Savage Press catalog

Talk to us at:

Tel:1-800-READ TNR
(1-800-732-3867)
Fax: (715) 394-9513
email: savpress@delphi.com
See our Web Page at:
www.cp.duluth.mn.us/~awest/savpress

Visa or MasterCard accepted.

P.O. Box 115
Superior, Wisconsin 54880
(715) 394-9513

We are always looking for good manuscripts – poetry, fiction, memoir, family history, true crime and other genres. Send a synopsis and the first three chapters.

Other Books Available from Savage Press

Hometown Wisconsin by Marshall Cook

Treasures from the Beginning of the World by Jeff Lewis

Stop in the Name of the Law by Alex O'Kash

Widow of the Waves by Bev Jamison

Stop and Smell the Cedars by Tony Jelich

Voices from the North Edge by St. Croix Writers

Gleanings from the Hillside by E.M. Johnson

Thicker Than Water by Hazel Sangster

Mystic Bread by Mike Savage

The Lost Locomotive of the Battle-Axe by Mike Savage

Moments Beautiful Moments Bright by Brett Bartholomaus

Total Eclipse by Judith James